The Flayed One

The Flayed One

L.A. Detwiler

Published by L.A. Detwiler, 2021.

THE FLAYED ONE

First edition. August 12, 2021.

Copyright © 2021 L.A. Detwiler.

ISBN: 979-8201344313

Written by L.A. Detwiler.

Also by L.A. Detwiler

The Flayed One
The Journal of H.D. Wards
The Flayed One

Standalone
The Diary of a Serial Killer's Daughter
A Tortured Soul
The Christmas Bell: A Horror Novel
The Redwood Asylum
The Christmas Bell: Rachel's Story
The Arsonist's Handbook
Mr. Alexander Garrick's Traveling Circus

Watch for more at www.ladetwiler.com.

To my husband, for always believing in my dreams

It comes at night when the world is a dusty, quiet ball of forgotten memories. The thing of shrieks, of shrill, wanton fears makes its presence known while others, the lucky ones, dance in and out of lucid dreams.

Its origins are the whispered legends on the hearts of victims and the mouths of the curious. Maybe it was here eternally, something as mystic as the origins of humanity itself. Maybe it is a spawn of Satan or crime or lust. Perhaps it is something else entirely.

But when it comes at night, make no mistake: You will not be saved. For even if the tendril-like fingers adorned with razor blade claws do not gut you from mouth to belly, you cannot escape its wrath. It will burrow its existence into your deepest core. It mars your flesh with the distinct mark of its horror. It will become one with you in the sense that once you lay eyes on it, you will be sent down a whirling tunnel of madness and pain.

And then, when it all seems impossible, when it appears that sheer craziness has overpowered you, it will come again.

When the Flayed One comes for you, make no mistake.

You will not be saved.

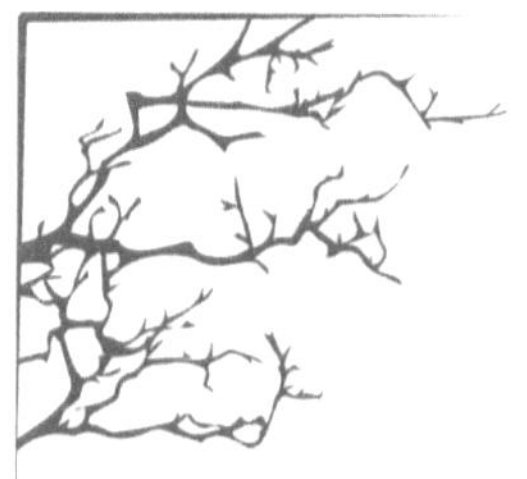

Chapter One

Her braids bounced down her back as she turned to slam the car door.

"Are you sure you want to go home that way?" the blonde behind the steering wheel asked, leaning out the window slightly to eye the other girl.

Mia Rose didn't lean down to peer in the window in a way one does to foster intimacy. She stood ramrod straight as she stared over the top of the peeling tan Chevy.

"I'll be fine," she assured. "Thanks for the ride." And without a single sentimental word or glance, she turned and headed to the forest refuge as Layla's car sped away.

The reasons for being dropped off in the dark woods near her house were twofold. First, her mother wouldn't be happy she was hanging out with Layla. In truth, Mia Rose wasn't happy about it either. But life unfolded in ways you couldn't predict or even contain. Still, she wasn't prepared for more hardships brought on by her parents' disapproval.

The second reason she wanted to be dropped off in the Redwood Forest was that it was her secret sanctuary, a place where she could go for inner calming she found nowhere else. Most of the kids in town avoided the eerie darkness of the woods because of the legends, the myths that haunted the town. Some avoided the woods simply to avoid the Redwood Psychiatric Hospital that bordered the woods, the spooky stain on the town's decidedly imperfect history.

For Mia Rose, though, the woods, even menacing ones, were a comfort. There was the isolation that permeated there, a dark sadness whistling through the trees that echoed her moroseness in the whipping wind. There was a paradoxical comfort in the misery when one was alone in the middle of it all. It was the only relief she experienced, her crestfallen psyche now an indelible stamp on her character. Mia Rose's feet plodded down the familiar yet untamed path towards home, the dense foliage absorbing the shockwaves of the devastation she radiated.

She ambled onward. Darkness promised to envelop the area soon, but she wasn't afraid. She knew the path by heart from her various travels down it last summer. Last summer—with her.

The memory simultaneously awakened a joy and a gut-wrenching pain within her. Last summer was a different time completely. Mia Rose was different. Everything was.

Her parents would be worried about her since she'd been gone so long. All they did was worry now, though, in their superficial way. Even when they were asking her about school or dinner, their faces were plastered with the condescending scrutiny she knew would never disappear now. She had awakened in them veracity difficult to abandon. From all that she'd been through and their reactions to it, she'd realized the harsh reality that love was never unconditional. Thus, Mia Rose wasn't in a hurry to get home to the inquisition, the disapproval, the pity in their eyes coupled with condemnation. So, as she stood amid the trees that seemed to stretch from hell to heaven, she veered right instead of left at the crossroads she'd marked before. Towards their spot she went. Perhaps she was a masochist. Maybe a piece of her wanted to wallow in sadness, to remind herself she could still feel after being dead inside for so long. Or, in actuality, she just needed to grieve the circumstances she couldn't openly weep about. Her feet followed the path to the tree trunk they had found last year during their explorations. She smiled, remembering the stupid joke she had made, the way her long hair billowed in the breeze as she ran playfully ahead.

As Mia Rose approached the spot, her hands started to shake and she crumpled to the ground. She didn't need to look in the box tucked in the hollowed-out trunk. She knew what treasures, what mementos rested in the time capsule hidden in the forest floor. She'd thought about adding to it last week, but the nail polish still sat underneath her bed. It was too hard to keep building those memories alone. It hurt too much.

Mia Rose let the tears fall wildly as darkness fell. She'd never been afraid of the night, preferring the blackness to entomb her in a way that could hide her from all viewing eyes. The darkness was a friend, holding her with arms of acceptance the daylight never could.

She swiped at her tears. "I miss you," she whispered into the air.

A moment of reverence passed, the trees gently blowing as if to fan her sorrow. Suddenly, though, a shriek, shrill and piercing, echoed in the distance. She thought in her wayward heart it was a sign. She didn't believe in a higher power, but she admittedly had a penchant for all things universe and nature. A sliver of her shredded heart craved a sign she was still there. The sound intensified, and her head instantaneously started to throb like the worst migraine she'd ever experienced. She scrambled to her feet, shock and confusion whirling her about in a roller coaster of messiness. The cacophonic sound continued, and soon it was accompanied by a putrid stench.

In her time in the woods, she often came across death. Carcasses of squirrels, of deer, of a bear once. This was different. This pungent smell of decay was accented by notes of charred something or other, by rotten eggs, by vomit. It was a smell she never had detected before in her seventeen years of life.

Mia Rose had withstood so much—but suddenly, she was overpowered by it all. The forest hideaway wasn't a welcome retreat anymore. The urge to return home incited her to get away. She suddenly didn't care so much about her mother's judging eye. She wanted to be in the safety of her bed, cocooned in her blanket, smothered by warmth and grief all the same.

Using her phone as a light, she turned around, the desolation and eerie sensations engulfing her. She scanned the tree line for the path that would take her to her house. It was not really a home but offered more security than the forest at the moment. But as her light panned left to right, she jumped.

Something was in the trees. A tall, slender figure. With her light shining, she only caught a glimpse of it moving in the other direction. Nimble and swift, it was gone before she could decode the sight. She shivered. The way it had moved, the slice of it she had seen. Her mind couldn't process it. Had it been a deer? Some kind of a wild dog?

No, it was much too tall to be one of those. Her mind raced for an answer, but her senses were still ringing from the smell, the sound. Both sensations mercifully faded now, allowing her head to clear. She didn't stop to ponder it any longer, though, rattled from the events. Instead, her feet dashed toward the path, moving solely from instinct and terror.

She didn't stop her graceless stumbling through the wooded path until her feet reached the grass in her front yard, until the porch light was in view. Heaving, she halted under the moonlight to look at the peeling white shack that represented so much to her—a place to rest, but also a place that made her restless. Life was an oxymoronic cluster, she'd come to understand. Still, turning back to the forest, she thought of the odd wail, the destructive odor.

There had been stories about those woods, the ones that drowned their house in a sea of darkness. As a little girl, she'd always implored her parents to lock the doors and the windows, to buy her a guard dog because the stories at school terrified her. She'd wake up in a cold sweat, terrified by the prospect of a deranged lunatic breaking into her house to chew on her bones and scratch out her eyes. Or, possibly even more horrifying were the stories of the spirits that wandered the grounds, tortured at Redwood Asylum and out looking for revenge.

Her parents, as parents do, assuaged her fears with tales of reality and safety. The Redwood Asylum was five miles away through the forest. No lunatic could maneuver those woods. In fact, there were reports of several patients, teenagers, and even nurses being forever lost in the thick density of the forest. She should be more afraid of traveling out there and getting lost in the woods than of an escapee attacking her.

For a while, the fragile words worked. They calmed her enough to let her bask in sleep, the peaceful variety. But as she got older and learned what all inhabitants of the area learned—that Oakwood, the neighboring town, had too many secrets to house solely in its borders, her fears resurfaced. The nightmares returned. And with them, the anxieties that no longer seemed so irrational.

Those woods had evil secrets. Oakwood had evil secrets. And the Redwood Asylum, harbored in the dense forest, had a wicked past that wasn't as protected as some thought. They were all living in a place where horror was bountiful, the real horror that resided in the world. A horror that cold destroy you, chew you up and spit you out as an ashen pile of bones.

Thus, as Mia Rose peered into the woods surrounding her, she knew there was darkness there, a vivid, omnipresent evil that enshrouded the house. If she wasn't careful, it might suffocate her, too, and entrap her in her own asylum of sorts.

She marched forward. For the first time in a long time, she wasn't thinking of the incident as she often did. She was focused now on the omnipresent risks surrounding her. Mia Rose supposed that was at least something.

It was something.

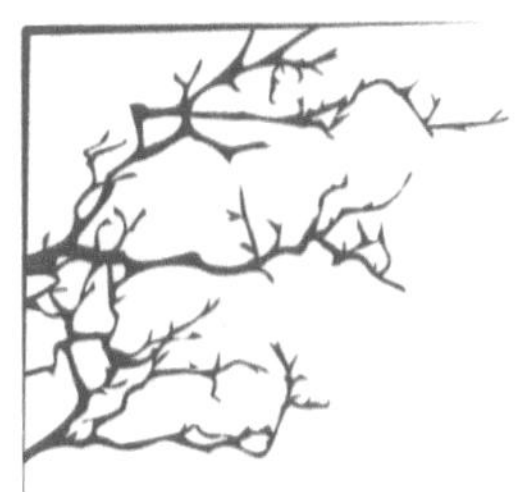

Chapter Two

I *shouldn't be doing this.* She reprimanded herself as the backpack slapped against her sweat-dampened back. Onward she trudged, never looking back. There were so many things wrong with what she was doing. Her parents would be furious when they found out she'd skipped school. They'd accuse her of backtracking. There would be hell to pay.

Still, as her braids slapped against her back and she marched on, she thought about how good it felt to rebel again. To be who she was. To choose her own path. *Screw them all, anyways.* Her parents, her teachers. The kids at school. They didn't understand her, couldn't possibly. It was part of the reason she left. It was their fault, she thought as she often did. It was all their fault. Resentment stewed within. Still, there was more to consider than her parents. There was last night, that odd sensation. What if the legends of the town were true? What if the woods really were dangerous?

She shivered at the memory of the night before. She'd tried to tell herself she was just imagining it all, that her overly active imagination had painted a tale to distract her. Darkness plays tricks on even the soundest psyche. Nevertheless, she knew it wasn't the case. If she closed her eyes and breathed in, she could conure the ungodly stench as if it still clung to her nostrils.

Something was out there. And against all the parts of her body screaming for her to stay safe, she wanted to find it. She ducked under a low-hanging branch, a rogue twig still stabbing into her bare legs. It stung, but she kept going. Discovery was pain. It felt good to know she was still alive in a sense. She welcomed the burn and the blood of the tiny cut.

The mission to explore had become vital to her being as the night passed. The more hours placed between the chilling moments alone in the woods and safety, the more her curiosity grew. Like Alice in a twisted Wonderland, Mia Rose hungered for something interesting, something fantastical, something consuming, even if it threatened her safety. Thus, when her mother barked for her to get out of bed at the crack of dawn, she knew she wouldn't be going to school. They always left first, Dad to the factory and Mother to the dowdy office job downtown. Mia Rose got the bus on her own for school. Not today, though. Today, she would choose her own path and chase her own whims.

Her nostalgic mind wandered for a moment, but she reined it back in. She couldn't think about that now, or it would derail everything. Mia knew a part of the adventure was about pushing down those painful thoughts. It was about focusing on something else for a while.

So she marched on, the dirt and leaves underneath her feet a welcome reprieve from the glassy linoleum and stares of her high school's hallways. They all were whispering about it, of course. They always would be. She would forever be the girl who was a stain on the school, the town, her family's reputation. Her entire life would be marred with questions of "Did she?" and "How?" and "Her fault?" Even if others weren't saying it, her battered mind was.

She could barely stand to be in her skin most days.

The search would most likely be fruitless, but it was still better than the pointlessness of walking the hallways and pretending nothing had changed. *Everything* had changed for her. She needed to reconnect, thus, with the Mia Rose of the past, the wild and bold girl she was just last summer—it felt like a lifetime ago, like another girl entirely. Still, she could recall a time when she was the girl who laughed in the middle of the field as lightning struck. The girl who wasn't afraid to be set on fire because she knew she could rise from the ashes. In short, the girl she was before it happened. The maniacal it that was a wall between before and now.

Silence coated the forest around her and plastered it in a somber quality. It didn't feel so wild here. But the way the world seemed to stop spinning and tilting out there wrapped her in a welcome cocoon. It felt like companionship to her weary soul. Warmth spread in her iced-over veins.

She walked toward the area she thought she had been in the night before, not knowing what she was looking for. If nothing else, she thought she could find their tree stump, sit for a while in the memory and the loss alone, free to grieve and to just be. She could rip off the faux smile she had to paint on—although admittedly not well— and sit in the ugliness of who she was now.

HER LEGS ACHED WHEN she reached the clearing. The tall grasses swayed in reprieve. She stood in the center for a moment, looking up at the sunny sky. Judging by the sun's position, homeroom was probably starting. Soon, they would know that she wasn't there. Would they call her parents right away? Would they even care, deep down? Would a piece of them, underneath the pretend mourning for her loss, be relieved she had seemingly disappeared? That their responsibilities had waned to freedom? She closed her eyes, swaying as the sunlight hit her cheeks. She thought of another time when the sun scorched her skin in a way that matched the burning within her. When the cool touch of friendly fingers offered solace she hadn't felt before.

She sighed, opening her eyes as a tear slid down. She spotted the tree trunk across the way and solemnly paraded toward the makeshift altar. The tree was more than just a hiding place, an adolescent treehouse for collecting prized possessions. It was more than a safety box to hide her stolen treasures from her mother's disapproving eyes. The tree stump had been theirs. It was a twisted shrine she had started when it all went to shit. And even though the forest scared the hell out of her last night, a part of her didn't care. It just felt good to feel something, anything. Even if it was sheer terror.

A moment of silence. A moment of peace. All was still.

Until it wasn't.

A snapping twig. She turned. Her heart chilled. The shrieking noise. The foul smell. It was back. In daylight this time.

The kids talked often of Raging Eddie, the lunatic who had escaped in the 60s from the Redwood Asylum. He was never found. It was just a story, though, one she'd heard since she the time she could understand the town's gory, not-so-distant history. The town was full of folklore to haunt, to chill, to warn. The shriek echoed again, though. Perhaps some stories were more.

Turning from the shrine, she dashed on as her bravado faded. Sometimes, she wanted to die. Now, faced with the unknown, she thought living wasn't half so bad. She sprinted faster, her feet finding the way in the daylight much easier. What a foolish idea it had been. She'd like to rationalize it all as her craziness emerging. It was all made up, a figment of a sick mind. She'd like to tell herself that those times they'd heard an odd noise or turned to see a shadow that was spectral-like, it was all imaginary.

But there were secrets in those woods, secrets bigger than an archaic asylum that was more prison than rehabilitation hospital. Perhaps that was what called to her. Secrets liked company, after all. She ran on, nevertheless, not ready to be a victim of the unknown just yet. Maybe eventually, but not now. She ran home under the beaming sun, her legs now used to the memorized route.

When she returned, her feet standing in relief on the familiar wood of the porch, she looked out into the vast stretch of trees. It was like she was seeing those woods by her house for the first time in her seventeen years of life. She wondered if this was what it was like for them, to see the familiar in an unfamiliar way.

She nodded at the image, slipping into a state of serenity.

But then, she screamed.

Fingers wrapped around her neck, squeezing until it, yet again, hurt to cry out.

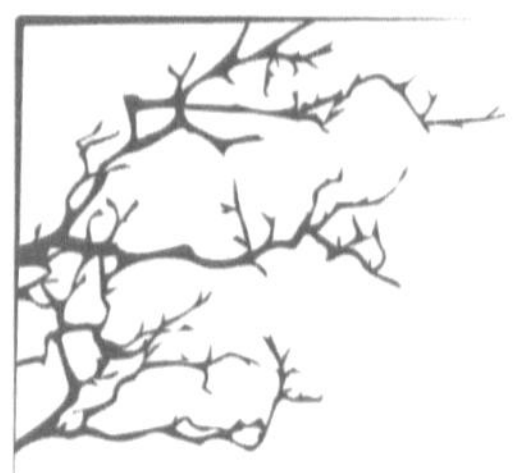

Chapter Three

"Where have you been?" the voice echoed as the fingers wrapped tighter around Mia Rose's neck. She could not answer.

Her mother dragged her into the house as the shock settled down. Her mother wasn't supposed to be home. Once inside the translucent protection of the indoors, the fingers released her. She sulked to the window and peered into the tree line, wondering yet again why she had even returned.

"Where have you been?" her mother vehemently repeated. Mia Rose turned around to face her. She knew the hatred would be stamped in her mother's eyes, the disapproval etched in the lines of her weathered face.

"Sorry," Mia Rose replied. Always sorry. Never enough.

"Sorry? I'm trying to do my job, and I get a phone call from the school that you're skipping? Don't you think you've caused enough issues this year?"

The girl shrunk into herself. She wanted to disappear.

"This has to stop," her mother chastised, studying her from across the kitchen with folded arms and her hallmark scowl. Mia Rose's eyes focused on the bulging vein that popped out from under her mother's mousey bangs. Mia pushed her hair aside. She'd abandoned those straight across bangs a few months ago, along with her signature blonde color. She'd opted for a dull black color that enraged her mother. Perhaps the woman realized it for what it was—a symbol that Mia Rose did not want to be a carbon copy of the pudgy, strait-laced woman. It was one of many choices that stamped her rebellion from being another girl in a long string of girls who cooked dinner for their husbands, went to church on Sundays, and valued obedience above self-expression.

"I know," she murmured, exhaling as her mother continued on a lecture about morals and disappointments and all the buzz words she'd been hearing for the past couple of years. Mia wished a part of her cared, that she could strum up a sense of guilt for what her mother was angry about.

That girl was long gone.

"Get to your room. Now. And so help me God, Mia Rose, if I find out you were out with that wild girl again," she murmured when her tirade ran out of gasoline.

"What? You'll what?" Mia Rose retorted, defiance bubbling deep within. What could she do now? The damage had been done. She'd already felt the sting of loss, of betrayal, of it all. Nothing her mother could do would be any worse now.

"Go. You're a disaster. A train wreck of a disaster. I can't wait until next year when you're gone for good. Just one more year of you, and then you can be out of here."

They were too far past the point of her mother's words hurting; she had learned over the past year that a mother's love isn't always permanent like the greeting cards would like you to think. Besides, it was the only thing she agreed with her mother about. It was the only connection they hadn't severed, this twisted wish that time could speed up and their paths could separate for good. Still, Mia Rose would never give her the satisfaction of admitting that.

One more year.

Maybe less if Mia Rose had her way.

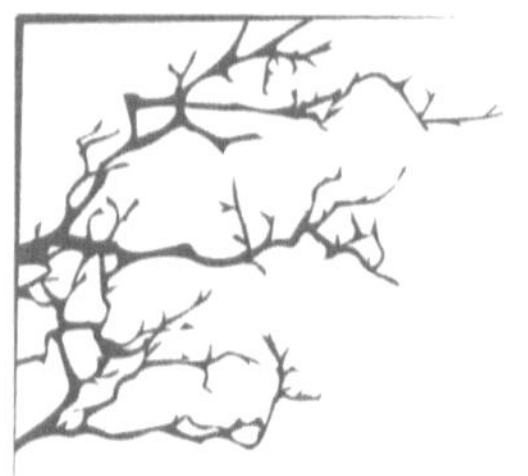

Chapter Four

M ia Rose eyed the saleswoman with disdain. The witch was going to ruin everything if she didn't stop staring. She ran her fingers over the bracelets, smiling sweetly at the woman with a nametag to distract from what she was about to do. Deception had become her strong suit in the past year or so, sometimes even to herself. When the dowdy woman finally turned around to handle a customer in the makeup department, Mia Rose casually swiped the rhinestone bracelet and shoved it into her pocket before slinking away.

Her eyes caught sight of a fancier, probably more expensive one as she exited, but you never took those. Too risky. It was easier to take something mediocre. That's what she'd learned. Mia Rose strutted out of the store without looking back. No one noticed her as she blended onto the sparsely crowded walkway.

Traipsing to the bus stop, she exhaled. The familiar rush wasn't there. What was the point if there was no one to share it with? Still, after the school bell rang earlier in the day, she knew she couldn't go home to the empty house. Now, she was alone, standing at a smelly bus stop in the early afternoon with a stolen bracelet in her pocket that meant nothing. It wasn't much better, admittedly. But at least it was something.

She considered stalling her return home. As depressing as this "adventure" was, it was still better than the cacophonous oppression that awaited her in the tomb of a house. Maybe she could cruise around town a little while longer, take in the not-quite-Mayberry sights but feel some sort of solace at being with others, even if they were strangers. At least strangers didn't have expectations from you, for you. She sighed.

No, she needed to get back—perhaps not home, but to the closest thing for her to a home. The sanctuary. The spot. She needed to drop off her latest catch. It was her version of flowers on a grave, she supposed. The stolen wares in the tree trunk were an odd remembrance, but they were all she had.

She boarded the bus, the stink of body odor and the stale remnants of cigarette smoke wafting about. Her fingers rubbing the smooth stones in the rhinestone bracelet tucked carefully away in her pocket, she thought of returning to the woods, of the shrill cry. The hairs on her neck prickled to attention. It was ludicrous, she knew. She'd lived by the forest her whole life. There was nothing out there other than a few packs of coyotes, some bears, and the distant moans of those imprisoned in the asylum. She shuddered at the thought of the stone place. She was no stranger to the horror stories of the institution. And as the bus finally screeched to a halt at the place nearest her home, she thought about how close of a call it had been.

She rubbed the bracelet again. Close wasn't exact, though. She was still standing, even if it was barely. Thus, she trudged forward to her forest shrine, to her solitude. She shoved down the ominous, foreboding presence in her chest as she diverted her attention to the trees. All would be okay, or as okay as it could be when life had come to a halt thanks to a horrific mistake. She was just manifesting the feelings of betrayal, of fear into those woods. Who wouldn't? It made sense that they would feel a bit haunted to her especially.

She paused for a moment, looking left at the path overgrown, the path she never took anymore. The red berries to the entrance taunted her, welcoming and sweet. She squeezed her eyes shut, though. *Don't think about it. You don't even know for sure.*

But she did. Deep down, she knew everything she needed to know. Her feet turned to take the path to the right. She was anxious to put any amount of space between herself and that horrid pathway to the left.

THE SMOOTH METAL CHILLED her fingertips as she anxiously and ceremoniously rubbed the jewelry, wandering to the tree stump. Her stomach churned at the sight that was paradoxically welcoming and unsettling. Looking at the stump that guarded all of their mementos from their wild adventures, Mia felt dead inside. She leaned over the stump, reaching in to grab the memory box. She didn't dare open it for the contents were enough to send her into a fit of tears.

She cracked the lid just enough to slip the bracelet into the dark void. She would not look at it again. Leaning on the rotting wood, she closed her eyes and breathed in the earthy scent that seemed to settle her. Here, when she closed her eyes and sucked in the smell of dirt and forest, she could pretend it wasn't now. Instead, in her mind's eye, it was then. She inhaled once more, knowing she needed to get back to her house. She didn't care anymore if her parents loved her or even liked her. But obedience, or the ruse of it, was easier than dealing with their anger. One more breath and she would go.

She opened her eyes and studied the empty clearing. For a moment, she thought she caught a whiff of that odor again, and her stomach fell. But it vanished quickly enough to assume she had conjured the scent. She turned to go the familiar way. Perhaps because she was standing there thinking of it all, she desired a new path. A different route unmarked by fated memories and terrors of before.

Thus, she turned right. Not toward the creek, though. Just a bit right, the path down the middle that they didn't usually like because of the prickly bushes and dense grasses that made the trail almost impassable. Mia Rose, though, thought it might be okay to get hurt. One foot in front of the other, she stalked through the tall, billowing weeds. Her foot plunged into a muddy spot, but the suction noise was satisfying in a way. She even smiled a bit as the jagged bushes scraped against her like a wild cat's claws. But as she clomped onward, looking down to steady her feet, she stopped as her gaze fell on something incongruous to the plants.

She blinked, then blinked again.

A leather-covered book of some sort, worn and ragged from the elements. There was an etching on the cover scratched in with a knife perhaps.

Her fingers traced the name of H.D. Wards, and paranoia settled in. She looked left, right, and behind her. Had someone followed her? Had someone known the whole truth?

She cracked open the journal, her veins bulging with the iciness of the unknown.

As she did, her eyes scanned the first page. Words hopped off the paper, assaulting her eyes and her mind. She couldn't read fast enough to satisfy her morbid curiosity. What was it? Whose was it? And why was it here? She glanced about again, unhappy that someone else had tainted their spot with their presence. She clearly couldn't count on being alone in their secret spot anymore, and she didn't like the thought of that at all.

Turning the journal over in her hands, she knew she should drop it back into the cushion of the weeds—someone might come looking to reclaim it. However, it no longer bothered her to take what wasn't hers. So she clutched the mysterious book tighter, a sense of foreboding claiming her psyche as she looked around and then looked forward. Curiosity plagued her as she wondered what story the pages would tell. Judging from the phrases she'd read, it would be a macabre one. In the far distance, a shriek pierced the air, but Mia Rose didn't heed it. Her mind was trained on the book in her hands, the mystery that somehow stirred a sense of life within her. It felt good to have someone else's secrets to solve.

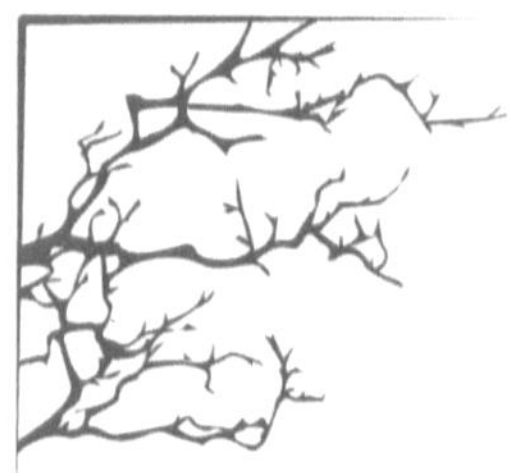

Chapter Five

There is truth in those wild tales. Because after what I saw, I say this—there IS something living in that forest. Last night, I saw it, whatever it was, slinking in the shadows.

I haven't been able to stop thinking about it, my mind clinging to it like an obsessive complex. The gaunt, slim finger slinking through the forest. The piercing cry it emitted. And the smell. Oh, Jesus, the smell, a corpse mixed with mildew, an earthy smell mixed with decay. Vomit rose in my throat and my heart almost exploded as I pulled Dorothy Mae back towards her house.

~The Journal of H.D. Wards

***

As Mia walked down the dusty path toward her grandma's house, two thoughts flooded her mind.

1. It was odd that the H.D. mentioned Dorothy Mae. Her grandmother's name was Dorothy. Could it be related to her somehow?
2. This must be how Red Riding Hood felt, traversing the woods oblivious to the big bad wolf lurking in the shadows. However, Mia Rose was relatively certain now a monster did exist that was much less pleasant than a wolf.

She'd stayed up all night perusing the journal, devouring every single word of the boy named H.D. She couldn't get enough of the chilling journal entries, of the accounts of a being inhabiting the forest. Who was this H.D. kid, and why was his journal tossed in the woods? And why had she only found it now? So many questions plagued her as she forced her feet to move forward, her eyes darting about.

Something was living in the forest. Sure, they'd all heard the stories. Even H.D. mentioned lunatic Eddy, a supposed asylum patient who escaped decades ago. Kids told stories of how he gnawed on human bones in the woods, how he'd sharpened his teeth to a point, how he had evolved to master night vision and could snatch a victim without them even knowing. Mia Rose had also heard the stories of the various disappearances in town. They were always chocked up to runaways or kidnappings—but the kids always talked about how the woods were known to digest wanderers. It had yet to spit any of them back out.

She had never been afraid of those woods, however. Growing up beside the Redwood Forest, the trees and nature sounds were always a harbor for her when the world was too much, when she didn't fit in—which was undoubtedly a frequent occurrence, even before last summer. When life got to be too much and she was struggling with her parents, with school, with her peers, with herself, a quick jaunt into the trees soothed her. She never felt terrified in those woods—until now. Because now, the words of H.D. made her question it all.

It was silly, she knew. Probably just the ramblings of some weird kid or an overactive imagination at play. Hell, maybe someone in town was playing a trick on her. She was the aloof kid at school, and after the town got word of what happened last year, maybe someone just wanted to amplify the cruelty the universe had dealt her. People sucked, as she'd come to learn.

The journal burned in her backpack, imploring her to indulge a while longer in the words. The secrets bubbled within the pages, waiting for her to solve them. Even if it was all rubbish, it felt good to focus on something new. It felt exciting to have the key to a mystery bigger than herself. In some inexplicable way, she had a purpose again. Deep down, though, it also felt terrifying to know perhaps there was validity to all the myths and legends circulating through the town.

She trudged on, the birds' buoyant chirping in the trees sharply contrasting to the dark terror housed in the words of the journal. She brushed it all off, not wanting to cloud her visit with her grandma. She would keep it secret for now until she figured out more details. No need to worry her grandma needlessly since she already was struggling.

Mia Rose let herself in the squeaky screen door like she always did. Edmund, her grandmother's huge Great Dane, barked and growled until he recognized her. Then, he was all over her, jumping wildly despite her protests and almost taking her down. Her parents had tried to talk Grandma into getting rid of Edmund in her state, but the woman refused. Mia Rose appreciated that.

The dog finally calmed and followed her deeper inside the home where her grandmother lived—and in some ways, Mia Rose, too. The girl glanced about to take inventory of the place. She knew how bad things were now, but a piece of her still expected to turn and see her grandma in her signature pink apron whipping up a pie or a meatloaf. The woman loved to cook and bake. Mia's childhood pudge that carried into her teen years could probably be blamed on the woman's penchant for cooking.

Instead, the house smelled stale, stagnant, and medicinal. Floral aromas that marked Mia Rose's memories of the place were replaced with an antiseptic smell. The oxygen machine beeped from the corner of the living room. Mia Rose wandered into the room where her happiest childhood memories occurred. Her grandma sat on the faded plaid couch, her pallor faded and concerning. Her condition was no longer shocking, but Mia's stomach fell every single time she saw her. Still, the television blared as it always did. Her grandma slurped on a bowl of chicken soup, her favorite. A sense of normalcy fought through the cracks.

"Mia Rose, dear, I didn't know you were coming today," she said, her face alight as she paused from the soup.

"It's Saturday, Grandma."

"Is it? I've lost track."

Mia claimed her seat on the faded floral sofa. She stared at the talk show Grandma was watching, thinking about all the summer afternoons she'd sat right here, watching the corny soap operas while Grandma fed her gargantuan lunches. There was always dessert after, too.

"Soup, dear?" Grandma asked, but Mia Rose shook her head. The woman's hand shook, and she thought about how much had changed in the last year. How the diagnosis had seemed to suck the life out of the vivacious woman who was more mother to Mia Rose than her own. How right in the middle of trauma, the universe piled more on with her grandmother's illness.

"I'm fine, Grandma. How are you feeling?" she asked, knowing the answer and hating herself for asking the pointless question.

"Like a piece of rotten cabbage, in truth. But I'm okay. How are you doing?"

That was Grandma. Always more worried about others than herself, even amid a terminal illness that certainly was causing pain.

"I'm okay, Grandma," she lied.

Grandma turned to eye her with the signature look she always gave when she knew Mia Rose was lying. She knew her tell—too well.

"Okay, I'm struggling a little bit. Mom and Dad have been on my case about everything and I'm just so sick of it."

Grandma sighed, setting the soup bowl down. "In their own way, Love, they're trying to protect you, even if it doesn't always feel like it. And even if I don't agree with their methods. Your mother's always been a bit—icy. She means well, she does. I have to believe that."

"By trying to make me something I'm not?" Tears stung her eyes, the inner, anxious child emerging. Grandma patted the couch closer to her, and Mia Rose leaned in. The child quieted.

They sat wordlessly. Grandma didn't have to say anything. She never did. From the time Mia Rose was a little girl, she knew the house down the lane where her grandma lived was comfort, pure and simple. There was no judgment there. Just warmth and love. It was why Mia couldn't bring herself to leave, even when she felt like it. The thought of running away and starting over had tempted her more and more as the months passed. Still, when she thought about her grandma, Mia Rose knew she couldn't do that. It wouldn't be fair to the woman who had done so much for her. She wouldn't worry her in what were probably her final days.

She'd considered moving in with her grandma, partially to escape her horrid house and partially to care for her. But she knew there were a lot of problems with the situation. One, her mother would never allow it—there had always been animosity between her mother and grandmother, deep-rooted in the past and antagonized by the fact Mia Rose loved her grandmother more. Her mother's jealousy over their closeness burned blatantly anytime there was a mentioning of her. The other issue was grandma. For although she would love to have Mia Rose there, she also was in a state where any independence she had left was crucial to her happiness. She would cling, kicking and screaming, to the fact that she could take care of herself. The timing would make it obvious, and she would argue that Mia Rose didn't need to take care of her.

So she did the best she could, visiting as often as she could. Her mother stopped in from time to time, too, but Mia Rose never went along for those visits. The iciness between the two estranged women was always exacerbated by the girl's presence, the jealousy uprooted again and again. They had two separate relationships with the elderly woman, and Mia Rose was fine with keeping it that way.

But she knew that if she took off, if she left town, it would be the final nail in her grandmother's coffin. She couldn't do that to her, no matter how badly she'd wanted out of the situation. She would be strong for her grandma. She owed her that much. She couldn't just give in and disappear, no matter how hard it got. Not yet, at least. She shuddered to think of the sadness that would be a precursor to any sense of freedom, any opportunity to leave. Mia Rose would endure a lifetime of her parents' wrath if it meant her grandma didn't have to die. Still, she knew bargains with the devil weren't hers to make. She would make the most of her grandma's final time. Then, when the dust had settled, she could make her getaway. If the doctors were to be trusted—which her grandmother was adamant they were thieving crooks—then there wasn't much time.

There wasn't much time left at all. The thought threatened to send Mia Rose into a fit of racking sobs, but she choked them back. She didn't want to upset her grandmother again with her tears.

They finished their visit, and Mia Rose kissed the woman's cheek, asking if she needed anything but knowing the response would be a resounding no. Even in her final months, Dorothy Mae was a strong woman. It gave her the courage to be strong, too.

She headed out the door, glancing at the woods again as a chill rattled her despite the day's warmth. The woods looked darker somehow, tainted. It was crazy how a few stories, a few words in a journal could change your perception.

But that was life. Always changing, and perception ruling everything.

She marched on, knowing what her next move would be.

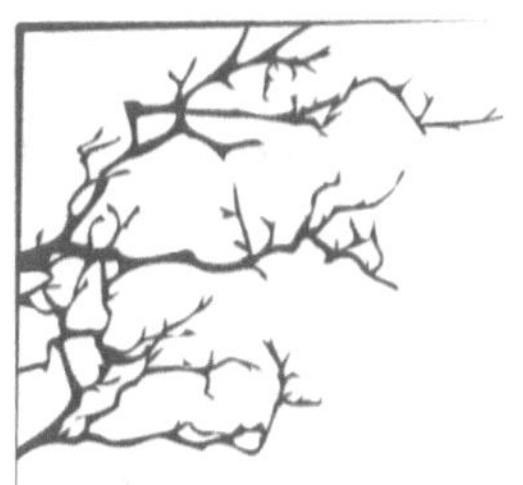

Chapter Six

The smell of paper, chemicals, and the librarian's overpowering perfume drifted in the chilled air of the library. As a girl, Mia Rose used to come to the library to escape the summer heat before her parents had splurged on air conditioning. Her fingers touched a row of children's books as she spotted a few favorites. Refocusing on the mission at hand, though, Mia Rose headed to the back of the library and planted herself in a seat. She sat straight in the hardbacked chair as she browsed the computer. Old Mrs. Tandry joined her a few moments later with the materials she had requested upon arrival. With her severe bun and sunshine yellow dress, the elderly lady was quite intimidating but also useful; she'd returned with the information from the archives that Mia Rose needed.

"I knew that boy, H.D. I thought the name rang a bell when you mentioned it," Mrs. Tandry mentioned when she handed Mia Rose the few articles they had available. "He disappeared a year before my family came to Cedarcrest. What piqued your interest after all this time?"

Mia blinked, thinking about the journal in her backpack. "My grandmother mentioned him. Thought I would do some digging. Curiosity, you know."

"Well, that's lovely dear. You ask me and the youth these days aren't curious enough. Always buried in their own selfish whims." Mia Rose exhaled as the woman walked away. She had a penchant for nosiness, so she was glad Mrs. Tandry had accepted her answer as truth.

Mrs. Tandry moved on to talk with Old Man Carlisle, the guy who worked at the post office. Mia Rose perused the files. An old newspaper article announced the birth of H.D. Wards in Cedarcrest on March 12, 1961. A few yearbook photos also were returned in the search. He had a dramatic combover, which made Mia smirk despite the circumstances. Finally, there was the newspaper article, a tiny snippet detailing his disappearance in the year 1972.

The parents of H.D. Wards noted he had exhibited odd behaviors in the months leading up to his disappearance, including ravaging his own arms and moody, hostile behaviors. H.D. was also noted as falling prey to hallucinations. Some friends of H.D. and teachers note that he had suffered from a drug addiction last year which had led to numerous criminal charges.

At this time, the police consider the disappearance a runaway. No evidence to denote the disappearance as a homicide or anything criminal has been detected.

Mia Rose chilled at the words. There was no mention of a journal. How hadn't the police found it? And why was it in the woods after all these years? There were always rumors of those woods beyond just lunatic Eddy. Some kids claimed a serial killer hid there. Mia Rose shivered as she considered the possibility. If that was the case, was he toying with her now?

She scrolled onward in the search of the archives, coming across more yearbook photos of the boy. Handsome, she thought, despite the combover and collared shirt. His eyes sparkled even in the black and white photograph. Her heart sank at the knowledge she had his last, troubled words in her backpack and that no one knew what happened to him.

His nonsense about The Flayed One, as he labeled the creature he came across, was probably just drug-induced ramblings if the newspaper was to be believed. He had fallen prey to addiction, and she simply had the ravings of a madman who disappeared shortly after.

Nevertheless, his descriptions were so eerie, so realistic. And what about the markings he described on his arms from the creature? The newspaper made it sound like self-harm—but what if it wasn't? What if after all this time she could be the one to discover what happened to him? She flipped past the sorrowful eyes of the boy she felt responsible for. And that was when she saw it in the next article. A tiny gasp echoed in the room, and Mrs. Tandry paused her conversation.

"Are you okay, Dear?" she asked from across the room. But Mia Rose had closed the file and was heading for the door.

"Fine. I just remembered something."

As Mia Rose strolled out of the building, the last archive swirled in her head.

This could change everything, she thought as she readjusted her backpack straps, squeezed her eyes shut, and headed for the sidewalk. She usually would take the shortcut from town through the forest, but today, she felt like giving it a wide berth. She wasn't ready to go home yet, the long way home, thus, calling to her.

Because if those final words of that article were true—

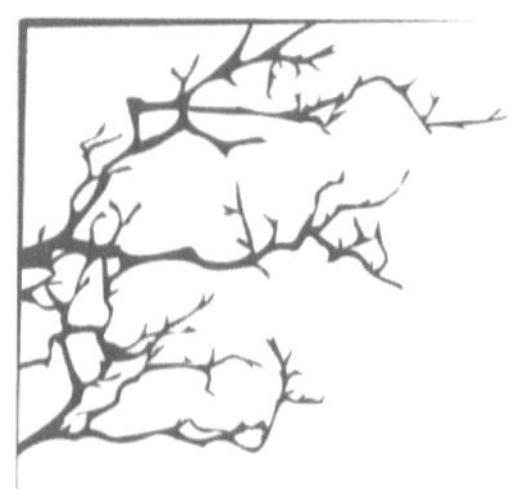

Chapter Seven

He lived in her house.

Mia didn't know why, but sitting on her front porch after dinner and rocking in the dingy, peeling chair, her mind froze on the single fact. It didn't matter she supposed. She should have known a boy wandering in those woods would have to live close. But if this was his house—and if his words were true—then the creature—

Stop it, she told herself. Nonsense. She'd lived in the house by the woods for seventeen years and never seen anything.

Yet, as she considered it, so did H.D. He was seventeen when it came for him. And then her mind settled on something else entirely. She shivered.

She should chuck the journal, forget it existed. She should write H.D. off as a crazy drug addict like the whole town did back then. She had enough misery to deal with. Still, she knew she couldn't do that. She was involved now, curious. More than that, she was desperate to focus on anything else—even if it was dangerous. Why was she so worried? What did she have to lose, anyway? Her parents despised her, but in a cold, formal way that kept her clinging to hope things could change. Everything she cared about was gone from her reach. Life was a shitstorm of sadness. Staring out into the darkness, she wondered about what was out there. About what she'd missed.

And so, Mia Rose made up her mind. With the words of the journal guiding her, she made the decision she would venture back out into the forest and find the spot where the journal was. She would look for clues, for answers that may or may not be found.

She had to try, though.

This time, she would try.

THE STICKY AIR MADE it hard to breathe as she marched onward, the familiar path underfoot. Twigs snapped as branches scratched her skin. One higher branch came precariously close to her eye. The darkness made it difficult to navigate, but she'd traveled the path so many times, she trusted her body to blindly make its way through.

Her parents were finally asleep. She didn't want to arouse any more suspicions or answer any more questions. Her life was an icy mystery to them, more now than ever. She wanted to keep it that way.

The words of the journal echoed in her head to the rhythm of her steps.

When the Flayed One comes for you, make no mistake.
You will not be saved.

A gloomy sense of foreboding infiltrated her, yet Mia Rose went on. Sometimes in life, you didn't have a choice, she knew. You had to keep going. Her investigative legs had been stretched, and she knew she couldn't just forget about it all now.

The journal was in her left hand. She clung to the scratchy leather cover as if it were her lifeblood. After a long, uneventful trek, she came to the spot. She shoved aside the final tree branch that guarded the sacred yet unremarkable place. She inhaled deeply and stepped into the clearing, the tree stump nearby her only comfort.

Silence rang out through the clearing.

All was calm.

She didn't know why she'd expected otherwise, as if some great reckoning would occur now that she had the journal. She gripped the leather-bound book harder as she mocked herself silently for thinking anything would be different. She'd allowed herself to be wrapped up in some escapism horror like a twisted girl. Glancing around, she inhaled the night air. It somehow seemed thinner here. She felt herself relax into a state of wonder, looking up at the night sky visible from the spot.

She felt ridiculous, but she had come for one reason. Thus, she pushed herself forward in the clearing, heading towards the path she'd taken with the prickly bushes. She started down the path, looking for the spot where she'd found H.D.'s words. It was hard to configure the spot in the darkness, but she meandered through the tall grass. It was a regular night in a regular wood. Nothing spectacular to see. In a way, she found disappointment setting in. Although H.D.'s words were terrifying, they were scary in an intriguing way. It had given her something to hope for—that fantasies could exist. And if monsters and legends could be real, after all, other possibilities opened up in her heart, too.

Her feet stalked through the tall grass until her eyes recognized the spot she thought was right. She held the journal out as if to eye it in the space to make sure it was there. She glanced around, even leaning down to pat the ground where the journal had been. She didn't know what she was looking for, but she had to try.

As she was straightening herself, though, and preparing to resign from the mindless mission, a snapping of twigs and a stomping on the ground startled her. She stood corpselike in the center of the crowded, overgrown trail, her hand gripping the journal with a ferocity not expressed as of yet. Her knuckles ached as the skin stretched. She scanned the area as her chest constricted, turning around slowly as her breath quickened.

As she turned back toward the clearing, her breath caught.

But nothing was there but silence, stillness. She exhaled loudly in relief, shaking her head at her erratic behavior and irrational worries.

But before she could calm her beating heart, it happened. The ear-splitting scream. She pressed her hand and the journal against her ears, trying to block out the shriek that rattled her entire body. The best way she could describe it was an anguished scream, yet even that wasn't quite right. It was soul-gutting, a decibel like none she had ever experienced. It was a screeching car wreck that went on for miles mixed with the pain of a wounded animal. It was part humanistic and part animalistic, inciting her to crumple to the ground despite all instincts telling her to run. As the scream blasted through the woods, another sensation mauled her—a smell.

Once, as a child, her pet hamster had died in the ventilation system. She could close her eyes and remember that scent like it were present any time she called up the memory.

This was fifty times worse. It was that distinctive odor of death but meshed with a salty, sulphury wasteland type of smell. There were odd notes indescribable. It made her dry heave over and over. Racked as she was by the smell and the sound, she acknowledged one thing for sure, even in the middle of the harrowing experience.

H.D. hadn't lied. His observations were true and real.

She needed to escape.

She found courage and strength to stand up, her eyes in a frenzy as they tried to land on the opening, the path that would take her to safety. She'd never been one for physical fitness; other than her nature jaunts, she wasn't one to go for a jog or to stay in prime condition. However, now she knew her life depended on it. Her legs carried her as if she were a feather.

Dashing through the forest, she told herself to keep going despite the migraine and nausea. Her house was not a haven, but suddenly she wanted nothing more than to be there on the peeling porch surrounded by her parents' questioning stares. Her legs ran on, the journal in her hand still as she covered both ears in a futile attempt to save her senses.

Her feet grazed the entrance to the path home. Twigs snapped to her left, something rushing through the foliage. Her legs ached and burned from the violent scratches all over them now. She ran faster.

Then, as quickly as it had started, the sound stopped. The relief from its expiration jarred her although she was relieved it had ceased. Her shallow breaths echoed through the night as her hand clutched to her chest now, trying to still her erratic heartbeat. On she went. But then, as she was rounding the familiar bend near the clearing, she stopped, almost colliding straight into it.

Her eyes were adjusted to the darkness, but it still seemed to blend in with the night somehow. Panic told her to turn around, to save herself. But for a moment, she paused, the being pointing its long, twig-like finger at her. The digit was armed with a chillingly pointed claw. Its face was not quite human, not quite beast, which confused her already overwrought brain even more. The smell was wave after wave of disgust. The sound began ringing in her brain again although the being did not seem to open its twisted, melted lips.

Overwhelmed with fear, she told herself to run but couldn't seem to stop staring, like a moth drawn to that deadly flame. Perhaps the most horrifying aspect of all was how it stood stone still. It didn't make a move to chase her, to grab her, to end her like it clearly could with its claws. It was calm, tall, unwavering as if to say it could take its sweet time with her. Its flapping, melting skin hung in sheets off of it. The ugliness of its marred, pocked skin made her turn up her nose.

The Flayed One. The phrase echoed in harmony with the shrill shriek. It fit. It just fit somehow.

Gathering her wits about her, she turned, terrified to have it behind her but having no choice. Suddenly, she wanted nothing more than to escape the woods, to keep breathing. Suddenly, life seemed worthwhile again. Worth preserving despite it all.

Mia Rose ran back on the path, her ears attuned to every branch falling, every twig snapping, every rustling leaf as she realized the horrid noise had again stopped. She didn't hear anything. The silence freaked her out, though, because she knew at any moment, it could blast in front of her and slaughter her. She charged through the clearing to the other path. The bad path. The one she never went to. She had no choice. *Sometimes, you have no choice.* It was a fact she had to swallow. Thus, she did not stop to look at the roiling creek beside the path or think about the consequences. She kept dashing, praying to the universe or God or whoever would listen that she wouldn't die here, alone, with the mysterious journal in her hands.

Heaving for air and survival, she rushed through the forest with swiftness lacking grace. She pummeled through branches, ignoring the sting of wounds as they stabbed into her. She needed to live.

When the sight of her house broke her trancelike mental state, she exhaled. She did not let her legs slow, though, until they were on the porch. Homebase. The chase was done.

But this was no childish game of tag, she knew. She whirled around, leaning on the porch railing to inspect the tree line. Her eyes frenetically searched for that thing she had seen, a whimper emitted as she recalled its features. Had it followed her home? She leaned over the railing as if to get a better look, the journal still in her hand. Nothing. She didn't see a single thing. Over and over, she looked, left, right, up, down. Nothing.

Nothing but wilderness and an inky blackness marked by trees.

Still, she knew she was not home free. If H.D.'s words were true, which she had certainly found evidence to suggest tonight, then her problems were just beginning.

Chapter Eight

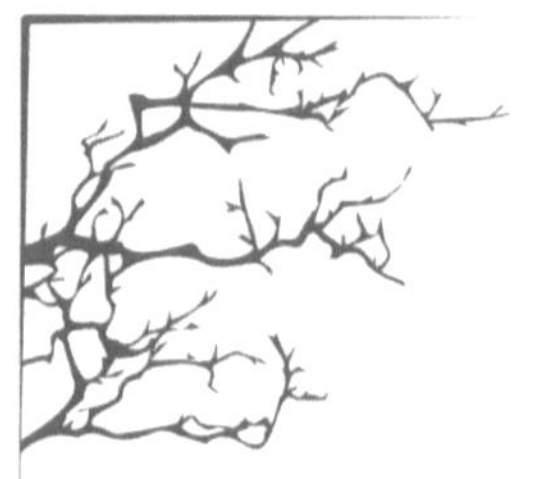

There's something living in those woods, all right. Something ominous, just like they say the grounds at Redwood are.

A smart person would steer clear of those woods like we've been warned to do since we were children. Like we've been scared into doing. But I'm grown now, and I've never been accused of being wise.

So I'm going to go back in. I'm going to figure out what the hell that was lurking in the shadows last night. I'm going to stuff this fear back down into the carcass of my being and figure out what the hell I saw tonight.

I'm going to find out what's lurking in Redwood forest, even if it kills me.

~The Journal of H.D. Wards, June 6th

Mia Rose did not linger on the porch long before seeking shelter inside. She popped open the front door and let it swing wildly, unconcerned about the ridiculous hour of the night, about waking her parents, about the trouble she would be in. It was too late now to worry about such trivial things. They all had bigger issues now.

She slammed the front door, locking and bolting it behind her before leaning her head on the wood and taking a breath. She collected herself for a moment before a thought panicked her. She crossed the room and peered out the window warily, half afraid the being would be there, its vicious claws waiting to annihilate her, to spread her blood all over the house in a final act of evil. Not long ago, she would've welcomed the reprieve from life. Now, she wasn't ready to meet such a hostile death.

A light flipped on.

"Mia Rose? Is that you?" the voice was confident and angry, not hesitant like most would be when awakened from a sleep. Her mother emerged in her robe, sleep lingering on her face but quickly replaced by another emotion entirely. She crossed her arms tightly in front of her slender yet worn body. Mia Rose's father stalked behind her, as though he were an afterthought.

"Where the hell have you been?" she asked, not waiting for an explanation from Mia Rose. The interrogation squad marched forward, her father taking a stance beside her mother in solidarity. "Good Lord, you look awful."

Mia Rose opened her mouth to explain, but nothing came out except a breathy cough. She couldn't find the words, her voice silenced by fear, adrenaline, and the knowledge everything she thought she knew had changed.

"What were you doing out there? Meeting up with someone new?" her mother continued.

"N-no, Mom, I swear. It's not like that," she managed to spit out, stalking to the kitchen and leaning on the counter in a faulty attempt to calm herself, to get her wits about her.

"Don't tell me what it's like, Mia Rose. Because all last year, you told me a bunch of lies. Do you know what that felt like, to find out that way? To find out what you were doing? And now here you are sneaking about in the middle of the night like some hoodlum. Were you drinking? Doing drugs?"

Mia Rose forgot about the monster in the woods momentarily. She saw only the monsters in front of her, the ones who never were on her side, who never let her explain. She stared icily at her mother as the accusations, the questions poured out. Her mother didn't even stop to allow her to get a word in, to defend herself. Presumed guilty was her mother's mantra these days, and Mia Rose despised her for it.

"And what about me?" Mia Rose shrieked, vehement tears stinging her already fragile eyes as she cut her mother's next rant off. "What about how I felt? Do you know what it's been like carrying the guilt?"

Her parents stood silent, staring at her. She bit her bottom lip to stop it from quivering. She wished at that moment she were more stoic, more unshakable. She did not want them to see how much they hurt her.

As the three stared at each other, all lost in their own worlds as they stood at an impasse, Mia Rose realized for the first time since the incident the guilt wasn't all hers to carry. It was theirs, too, to an extent. It was her parents for not accepting her, for not letting her be who she was. Mia Rose carried a lot of the blame, but they had played their part in the Shakespearean-like tragedy that had unfolded in those woods.

"This has to stop. You're almost a grown woman. What kind of life do you want?" her mother asked in a quieter tone.

It was a rhetorical question, a question Mia Rose was not expected or allowed to answer. Her mother knew what kind of life she should want. That was enough for her. That was supposed to be enough for Mia Rose. She had learned long ago that being cut from a different cloth, that having a different destination in mind, was not something the family supported.

Mia Rose thought about the monster in the woods, the danger they were all in. The words formed on her tongue. She wanted to tell them about the peril facing them that trumped everything else. She longed for them to hold her and tell her they'd fix it like they had when she was little and was afraid of the invisible monsters under her bed. She wanted for once in her life not to have to bear the brunt of the weight herself.

But some things are not to be, she knew. Looking into their fiery, judging eyes, Mia Rose understood she would get no relief from confessing to them the truth. She clung to the journal tighter, holding it against her side to not draw attention to it. Like so many things in life, she was on her own. They would be of no help. She would have to handle the situation while treading the waters of solitude.

"What kind of life do I want, Mother? One far, far away from here." She stomped past them to her room, knowing it was true. As soon as Grandma Dorothy was gone, Mia Rose would be gone, too. She would always carry guilt with her about what had happened in the town of Cedarcrest, about the part she'd played in it all. Still, she would carry the heavy luggage to another town, to another wood, where she would never be able to start over but she could at least start as herself. As she tucked H.D.'s journal away and stood staring out her bedroom window, she knew if she survived long enough to get away from the town, she would not carry any shame over what happened to her parents. They deserved the monster of the woods. They deserved to be taken unaware. Her heart cracked a bit more at the thought, but she was used to cracking. Her heart was splintered beyond recognition, so one more injury didn't even cause her to stir.

She spent the next few hours peering out the window, wondering if it would come back.

It *would* come back. H.D. had warned her. And she was on her own to figure out what to do about it.

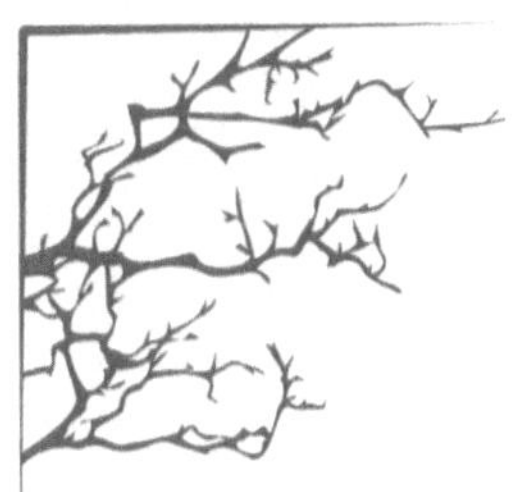

Chapter Nine

"I marched on. My feet stomped over brush on the forest floor. I inhaled and exhaled wildly but reminded myself to stay calm. I trudged onward so far, I feared I would be forever lost. Perhaps that was what happened to all those children, those women, that man last summer who disappeared in our town and in Redwood. My eyes glancing about, I realized everything looked the same in the darkness of the forest, but I suspected even in broad daylight, it would be a claustrophobic labyrinth of decay.

I had just convinced myself to turn around, to head home, when a wall of smell hit my nose. I inhaled and coughed, the scent doubling me over. That smell—God, it was indescribable. A burning, corpse-like smell that made one think of horrid possibilities.

I panned my flashlight about, realizing I had come to a bit of a let-up in the forest cover. A clearing of sorts sat empty, tall grass and the moonlight letting me breathe despite the smell. It was a sense of relief that flooded me in this circular field. The open air greeted me like a gift. How far had I gone into the woods? Why was there a sudden dissipation of trees here? The odd circular area sat still and undisturbed.

My nose covered with my hand in a bawdy attempt at preserving my stomach, I stood in the clearing, tears from the smell dripping from my eyes. It hadn't waned. Even in the open air of the clearing, the smell was the thing of nightmares."

The Journal of H.D. Wards

***

I t hadn't come that night. She exhaled in relief when she woke the next morning without a scratch, without a bad dream, without anything at all. She'd fought the good fight most of the night, trying to stay awake and stay vigilant. She had given into exhaustion, though, and the fact she was mostly dead inside anyway.

Still, when she thought about the being, its long, scraggly finger crookedly pointing, she wanted to vomit. She barely got down any food or coffee the next morning at breakfast, staring past her parents so as not to make eye contact with them but also so as not to take her eyes from the door.

It comes at night. That was what H.D. had written. But what if this time it was different?

"Don't even think about going anywhere after school," her mother barked, interrupting her fears. "Straight to school, straight back."

Mia Rose met her mother's words with a scowl. Grounded. A word she was familiar with these days. Her mother, though, didn't realize—Mia Rose had nowhere she wanted to go anyway. She chilled at the thought of stepping outside at all, pictures of the creature plaguing her.

In fact, when breakfast was over and her parents left, threatening her not to pull any crazy stunts, Mia Rose stood at the door's threshold. She considered walking to the bus stop like a responsible girl, going to school and doing what she was supposed to for once. However, the

40

sight of the tree line in the misty morning fog sent a chill right through her. She pictured the being, its melted skin and horrifying stance. She pictured the finger pointing at her, claiming her.

Still, she took a breath. It would come at night. She needed to be ready.

For now, though, she needed to do what she could to keep her parents on her side. She figured she might need them eventually, and it wouldn't do to have obliterated their trust in her even more than she already had.

She stepped out into the misty morning, inhaled, and crossed her fingers that H.D. was right, that the being of terror only came in the middle of the night so she could live one more day. At least one more day.

THE WIND HOWLED OUTSIDE, the moderate day turning to a tundra-like feel with the setting of the golden sun. Mia Rose wrapped her arms around herself, trying to constrict herself enough to halt her shivering. The quivering of her body, though, was as much from terror as from cold.

In the middle of the argument the previous night, it seemed like a prudent idea to conceal the truth about the creature from her parents. She stood tall and proud, too angry to ask for their help. In the daylight, her decision to handle the situation on her own seemed manageable.

Now, though, with the inky night enveloping her bedroom window once more and the terror of the unknown creeping into her bones, Mia Rose wondered if she'd made a mistake. She was not capable of protecting herself, her family, from the fiend. She was not strong enough or brave enough to stand strong.

What choice did she have? For all of the times she walked to her bedroom door and let her fingertips graze the knob, she had let reality pull her back. She could parade to her parents and tell them what she saw—but they would never believe her. Hell, she wouldn't, either. They would assume she was drowning in grief or manipulation or anything but the truth. She inhaled, frustrated, wondering how she found herself in such a damn mess.

Her eyes stared out the window, darkness also submerging her in her own room so she could peer out. And what if it came? What would she do? There was nothing to do, as H.D.'s words showed. She was doomed.

She thought about the razorblade in her nightstand. Just in case. Just in case things got unbearable. It was just a matter of pulling the drawer open. It comforted her somehow. It made her feel in control. She hadn't thought about that razorblade for months. That was something, she supposed. It was something.

She could end it now and save herself the agony. Still, the thought of her grandmother, of the pain it would cause her—it stopped her then. It stopped her now, too. Her parents might deserve a horrific death, but she did not. She could not let the creature get her sweet grandmother. She had to fight back. Her grandmother was fighting, was staying strong in the middle of unwavering odds. Mia Rose would have to rise up, too. She inhaled, finding that deep-seated strength she'd clung to viciously at one point but had lost slightly over the months. She dug deep, clung on, and stood stoically staring out the window.

The night went on. The wind howled.

It did not come.

Minutes ticked to hours.

It did not come.

She sat at her desk. Her eyes grew heavy.

It did not come.

The wind howled again. The tree scratched at the window.

It did not—

Mia Rose's eyes shot open. There was no tree branch outside her window. There was nothing to scratch at it, even in a windstorm. Nothing except—

The scratching continued. A tapping, rapping, scratching that jolted her soul. Her stomach caught in her throat, leaping and flipping like a wild animal escaping its hunter.

There was no raven at her shutter, there was no gentle beast. For when she outstretched her legs and found her way to the window despite every cell of her body urging her to run away, she saw it.

It stood staring at her with its vacant gaze that was both neutral and also claiming. Its face seemed to melt, the flayed skin almost floating off its face, its limbs, its whole body. It stared painstakingly at her as its long nail screeched down the glass, scratching and seemingly burning its etchings into the surface.

Mia Rose's screeching filled the house. She stumbled and scrambled toward her door, making her way to her parents' room. Nothing else mattered but getting away. Her shrieks had startled her parents awake, and they met her in the hallway to see what the matter was. Her words flung from her lips, her harangue confusing her parents who were still weary from the remnants of sleep.

"It's out there. It came. It came. We're doomed," she cried, knowing her words made no sense but desperate to make them understand.

"What are you talking about?" her mother asked, reaching for her in the first form of motherly love Mia Rose had experienced in almost a year.

"The Flayed One. The creature. It lives in the woods. It's outside my window. It wants to kill me."

Mia Rose watched her parents exchange a glance. Her heart pounded in her throat, her skin clamming up.

"What are you talking about?" her father asked, venturing into the territory.

"Go. I swear. Go. It's outside my window. The creature."

Her parents exchanged glances again, but they calmly walked to her room. Her dad inched toward the window, peering out. Mia Rose held her breath, terrified he would get too close to it, that she had sent him into his death trap. He leaned into the window. Mia Rose held her breath. Slowly, after a long moment, her dad turned around, her mother expectantly staring. The moment of truth, the weighing of the scales.

He shook his head. Mia Rose exhaled, shaking her head at the faulty verdict.

"It was there. I swear. I saw it the other night. It chased me. It followed me here. And I found a journal that talked about it. The kid who lived here before us, he saw it, too. It's dangerous. It's going to keep coming back for us."

Silence intermingled with the whistling wind outside. Mia clambered to the window, now desperate to see the being she so crazily tried to escape. Nothing. Blackness. She took a step back, holding her head. For a moment, she wondered if she had imagined it. If it had been a horrific nightmare induced by exhaustion, by the words of the journal. Minds could play wild tricks, she knew.

"Are you doing drugs?" her mother asked, a wispy quality to her words that made them seem even more pointed. Mia Rose whipped around.

"Of course not. I'm not lying. I'm not. We're in danger." Tears streamed down her face. For once, they needed to believe her, even if she did not deserve it.

Another glance. She read what they were saying with their body language, their facial expressions.

"You have to believe me," she cried, hating herself for the pleading quality to her voice. "You have to."

"We're going to bed. We'll talk about this tomorrow. Get some sleep," her father answered. They swiftly exited the room, shaking their heads, hushed murmurs floating in the air as they traveled down the hallway.

Mia Rose stood in the center of her hollow room, crippled, gutted by the fact she had known even before they came into her room—they didn't believe her. Of course, they didn't. They never did. They never saw her, never understood her. Why would this be any different?

She squeezed her eyes shut. She saw what she'd seen. She knew it was true. And H.D.'s journal held a similar story.

"DAD, GET UP," I YELLED into their room once I reached the threshold. I floundered into their sanctuary, shaking him from the precious peace of sleep until he was awake. He blinked, staring at me, but the words choked in my throat. I couldn't figure out what to tell him or how to make him understand the gravity of it all.

"There's something outside. There's something—strange—trying to get in. Please, get up." My words tumbled out in a frenzied string of terror. It took him what felt like forever to decipher them.

He sleepy wiped exhaustion from his eyes. I shook his arm.

"All right, all right. Calm down," he murmured, clearly in no hurry. In fairness, I had never been a stranger to nightmares. He probably thought I was having another episode.

Still, Mama sat up and pulled her robe around her tighter. She turned the lamp on as Dad followed me to my room.

My dad never believed in guns. There had been an accident when he was growing up with his cousin Vinnie. So even though we lived on the edge of a forest where bears, even coyotes roamed, we did not own a substantial weapon other than some knives. It had never bothered me or struck me as odd—until now. As my dad walked toward my window unarmed, I wished for nothing more than a gun.

Terror clung to my chest. "Dad, be careful. It's a creature. W-with claws. It's dangerous. Be careful." I tried to reach for him, but he continued toward my window.

I noticed the tapping, the scratching had stopped.

He crept toward the window, the darkness veiling him in a sad attempt at sneaking about. I held my breath, running my hand roughly through my hair as he inched forward. Tears welled in my eyes as horror ripped at my chest.

But when he got there and peered out, he stood silent. There was no scream, no shock. We did not bond over his verbalization that the creature I'd seen was real.

After a long moment, he exhaled.

"Son, there's nothing out here. It was probably a coon or something." And he turned back, his eyes wearing the frustration I'd seen so many times.

"No, wait," I murmured, rushing past him to stare out the window. I had seen what I had seen. I knew it was real.

But when I went to the window to prove it to myself, to my dad, I shook my head. Nothing but blackness, the emptiness of the forest enveloping the house as it always did. There was nothing there. It was gone.

"Maybe it's around the front," I protested, rushing out of my room, now more desperate to see the being again than to get away from it.

"Son, listen. Go back to bed. It's just one of your nightmares."

I whirled around. "It's not, Dad. It's not. I've seen it. It lives in the forest. It kills people. It has hanging skin and claw-like black nails and—"

"Enough. That's enough. We're not going down this path again, Son." His words were articulated with a shortness that startled me. His deep voice bellowed in the tense air between us. I clenched my jaw as he straightened his back. He stared defiantly at me, his son who had disappointed him in so many ways and who still was messing his life up.

For a moment, the dread of the being faded as I looked at the man whose love had become conditional. I couldn't blame him. It was my fault. I'd brought this on myself, cried wolf, and created so much pain in the family. Now, I was paying the price.

I would yet again endure solitude—this time, though, in the battle against a force unseen.

I didn't refute his claim. I didn't beg him to walk with me. I watched, instead, as he returned to his room and shut the door, leaving me in the hallway.

My back slid down the wall in the hallway as I tried to steady my shaking hands.

Was it still out there? Would it come back?

Fuck. I don't know what to do with this. All I know is I can't go back to sleep because it comes at night. It comes at night with its prying claws and lesion-covered body. It is a scourge in the forest, and now it has become a malady in my mind, in my life. I will never be able to make them see until it is too late. And even then, who will believe it?

~The Journal of H.D. Wards

***

Mia rose sat with her back against the headboard, her attention transfixed on the window. She hadn't imagined it. Neither had H.D. But if the ending of the journal was accurate, H.D. did not live long to tell the story. Only his written words survived. What would become of her?

She hated her parents for doubting her, yet she also understood where they were coming from. It was a fantastical story. She would probably have a hard time believing it if she hadn't seen it with her own eyes. Hell, she'd been quick to dismiss H.D. Wards as a madman, a psycho, a drug addict who was hallucinating. Why would her parents believe her, especially after the past year? Such was the difficulty of life, Mia Rose supposed. So many things you had to see yourself to understand—and the world was too vast a place to see it all through.

Darkness infiltrated her room. She thought about leaving the light on, but what good would that do? If it were to come, it would come regardless. There was no stopping it.

When the Flayed One chooses you, make no mistake.

You will not be saved.

She fell asleep with H.D.'s journal in her lap, open to the page that marked her doom.

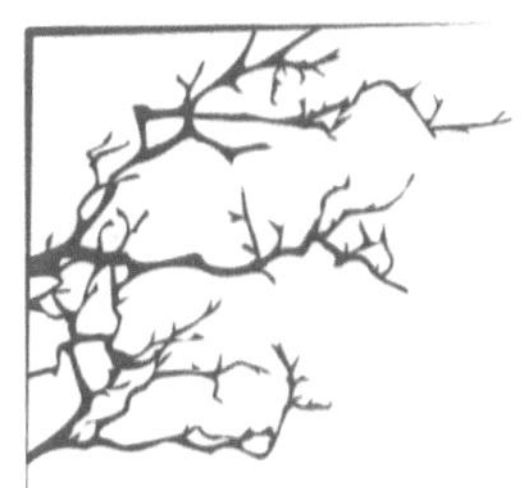

Chapter Ten

Her eyelids flipped open, and she gasped for air. Her body flailed as the burning, searing sensation in her arm prompted her mouth to open and shriek. The wail never escaped her lips, though—the skull-pounding sound echoed in her head, and the godawful smell obliterated her ability to reason. She squeezed her eyes shut, all of the sensations causing her consciousness to flicker.

Her arm felt like a hot tea kettle was planted on her skin, the stench of scorched flesh mixing with the decaying odor from before. This could be the end. She would die in her bed at the hands of the beast. How the hell did it get in? How had it snuck in?

She covered her left ear with her free hand, desperate to block out the mind-numbing sound that still pulsated around her. It seemed to come from her insides, deep within her ragged chest and mind. Its fiendish fingers squeezed tighter. The leathery texture of its skin made her shiver, the pain debilitating but the disgust at its touch worse. Despite the overwhelming noise and smell, Mia Rose fought unconsciousness. She flicked her eyes open a sliver, just enough to be aware of what was happening.

She instantaneously wished she hadn't.

In the darkness of the room, her gaze landed on the figure to her right. It hovered above her, its bony fingers furled tightly around her forearm, the pointed claws razoring into her skin. Mia Rose yanked away, vomit rising and panic encompassing her. The creature, however, did not move. It stood stone-still, its vacant eyes locked on her. She blinked and pulled, hoping against all odds she would awaken from a nightmare, sweat covered but unharmed.

She did not awake. She opened her mouth to scream, sobs leaking out despite the sense-defying horror. She struggled and flailed. It remained unwavering, indifferent, and strong. Her struggle made no impact. Its grip did not loosen. She closed her eyes again, willing the sound, the smell to stop.

And then, after what felt like an eternity in the inner circle of hell, it did. It stopped. All quieted. The sensations whisked away into the mystic night breeze.

The figure faded away into the night. Even before she opened her eyes, she could sense it had gone. It was like the thing was a part of her, an interlocked puzzle piece in the web of who she was. She wanted to pluck it from her, to forget it existed. Still, the piece stayed locked in, the ripples of the creature remaining in the aftermath. The aftershock drowned her long after she opened her eyes and ascertained it was gone from inky blackness around her. Her gaze darted about, checking every corner, every nook, every possible spot just to be sure.

It was gone. Vanished like a figment of her imagination.

Nonetheless, her arm still throbbed from its grip. Her hands shook as she reached out to touch the grooves from its claws that had pierced through her skin. Blood trickled, her tears dripping down her face mixing with it all. The sobs were silent coughs at first that morphed into racking, shrieking wails.

The light flipped on in her room. She shuddered.

"For God's sake," her father yelled. Mia Rose had wrapped her arm underneath her quilt. She didn't want to hear their doubts, didn't want to deal with their angry accusations. "What's going on?"

She wiped at her tears with her left hand. She left her bloodied, battered arm under the quilt, hoping no rogue drops gave it away.

"Just a nightmare," she whispered, wishing it was true.

He studied her for a moment, his mustache wriggling in condescension. She detected a slight shaking of his head. Then, he wordlessly flipped off the light and shut the door, leaving Mia Rose alone with the monsters that plagued her. Minutes ticked by. After many deep breaths and shuddering whimpers, Mia Rose regained a semblance of composure.

This happened. The monster is real. It will come back.

She repeated the phrases like a twisted mantra as her left hand stroked her burning arm. It grounded her in reality. She rose from her bed, hobbling to the chair at her desk. She stared out the window, tears dripping down her face as she wondered how things could get any worse. With her skin scorched and flaking, she rocked herself in her chair, thinking of painful memories from a time not so long ago. At least the physical pain of her arm now matched her internal status, she thought with a twisted sense of appreciation. At least there was that in what she feared could be her final days.

It had chosen her, after all.

It had clearly chosen *her*.

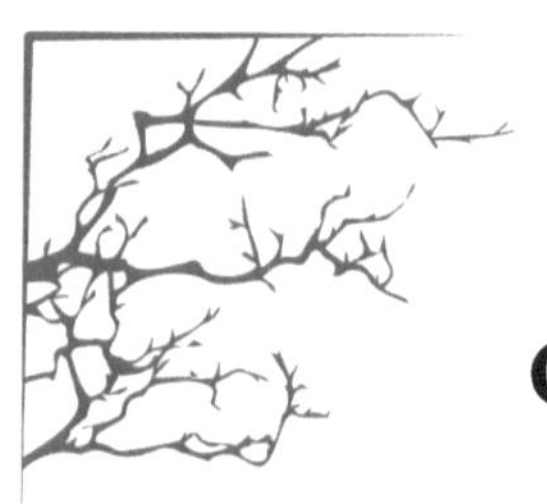

Chapter Eleven
Last summer

The bracelet weighed next to nothing, yet it still seemed to drag her jacket pocket down. It was like a blazing emblem of both shame and exhilaration. Mia Rose glanced down several times to see if there was a burning black ring in the denim of the jacket as if she were Hester Prynne—except her Scarlet A would be an S for shoplifting.

"Are you coming?" Lilly asked, turning back to look at her. The girl's wild, untamed red hair billowed behind her, a leaf stuck in it. Her words pulled Mia Rose out of her head, as they always did. She pushed onward, wondering if the earrings in the redhead's pocket were pulsating, too. She doubted it. Lilly Carlisle always had a reckless streak, a wild reputation in their town. It was why Mia Rose didn't tell her mother she was spending so much time with the girl.

They pushed onward, through the path. Mia Rose had no idea where they were going, but Lilly had insisted she knew exactly the place to go after their stint at the boutique in town. Mia Rose had been stunned by Lilly's perfect smile, her ability to make small talk, her penchant for distracting the elderly Mrs. Gentry at the jewelry counter just long enough to swipe a few items. It clearly wasn't her first rodeo. The fact didn't horrify Mia Rose. It excited her. She'd spent so many years fading in the background, the proverbial wallflower no one noticed. It felt good to run with a freer girl, a girl who liked to stir trouble and leave a mark in the world.

Mia Rose's legs ached. She had frequented these woods near her house as a child, always more at peace in nature than around people. But she'd never been out this far. A piece of her was a tiny bit afraid, after growing up hearing all the town folklore about crazy Eddie and all those other asylum stories. She would never admit it to Lilly, though, who hummed to herself as she jaunted down the path. Mia Rose blindly followed. She didn't want her to think any less of her.

It was crazy to Mia Rose that this wild child of a girl was befriending her this summer. They'd barely said three words to each other over the past two years since Lilly had moved into town. But a few weeks before school let out, their worlds collided thanks to a tedious biology project and an asshole named Richard Stevenson who was as chauvinistic as they came. Over their shared misery, however, the girls had noticed they had a lot in common—a love for old rock music, an obsession with poetry, and unrelenting boredom with their small town. Thus, when Lilly Carlisle asked if Mia Rose wanted to go to the mall that first week of summer, she was more than willing to throw herself into something she was a stranger to—friendship. True friendship.

"Almost there," Lilly yelled back, bringing Mia Rose back to the present reality. She trudged onward. In truth, she'd have followed Lilly anywhere. Even into the pit of death. It was why she hadn't batted an eye when Lilly handed her the bracelet. With a tingling of excitement, she'd shoved it into her pocket without a second thought.

Lilly pulled back a branch on the trail, holding it for Mia Rose. When Mia Rose passed it, she saw a clearing she hadn't known existed. She'd never wandered in this direction.

"It's beautiful here," she said, meaning it. The nature-loving girl deeply rooted within her smiled at the serenity of the scene, at the emptiness of it all.

"It's one of my favorite places. I come here to think, to just be," Lilly said, turning to look at Mia Rose. She smirked. "And also to hide my stash."

Mia Rose turned to her. "Really? You just keep it here?"

Lilly pulled on her hand, leading her to a tree stump that was hollowed out a bit. It sat in the middle of the clearing. She reached inside as Mia Rose watched. Out came a metal box that Lilly placed on the ground.

"My mother would kill me if she found out about all of this." Inside the box, Mia Rose saw several other pieces of jewelry, what looked like a camera, and a sparkly keychain. Lilly pulled the earrings and a bracelet out of her pocket and put them inside. She turned to Mia Rose, who extricated the bracelet from her jacket.

"I don't understand, though," Mia Rose said, handing the bracelet to Lilly who added it to the criminal time capsule. "Why steal the stuff if you aren't using it?"

Lilly plopped on the ground cross-legged. Mia Rose joined her. Lilly ran her finger over the rim of the metal box. A gentle breeze rustled the trees around them, but there was a quietude engulfing them that could only be found in the forest. Mia Rose breathed in and exhaled all she'd been holding in. She studied Lilly, the sunlight glimmering in her red hair in a way she knew she would always remember.

Lilly sighed. "I don't know. I guess it's just because I can. I know that sounds stupid. I don't want the stuff. I just—I like to know I can do it. Can leave a mark, even if people don't realize it. So many things in this world are out of your hands. Are done to you, not by you. It's something I get to do, something I can control. It's a piece of me that I own and no one can stop." Lilly looked up at her then. Her green eyes stared into Mia Rose, questioning but also recognizing. "It's stupid, I know."

"It's not." And it wasn't. It clicked for Mia Rose. Suddenly, she wanted nothing more than to fill their secret treasure box together. It was a place for them to showcase their work—but only for the two of them to appreciate. A secret connection shared by no one else.

"Look, I know we haven't been hanging out long, but you are such a breath of fresh air in this godforsaken town and life. Being with you, I just feel like myself. Everyone else just looks at me as this crazy redhead with weird dreams and a badass reputation to live up to. With you, I don't know. It's just peaceful."

"*I feel the same way,*" *she replied, smiling back at Lilly as she tucked the box into the tree trunk. They sat for a long while then, just staring out into the clearing. Neither talked. They just listened in the silence, recognizing a familiarity in their breathing that neither had found anywhere else. Mia Rose realized what she'd been missing all of her years. She realized that friendship didn't have to be some superficial, complicated thing like in the movies. It could just be sitting in a clearing sharing one's true self.*

Eventually, when they got up and dusted themselves off, they talked about the things teenage girls talk about. What Cassandra Adams was wearing yesterday. What they wanted to do after high school. The way Ricky Ranson had looked at Lilly when they were at the Shakes Galore stand the day before. They laughed and joked, traveling away from their treasures but knowing they'd be back.

Mia Rose went home that night knowing she'd found a place to call home, a place to let her hair down. And as she sat at the dinner table across from her straightlaced, stoic parents, she knew that Lilly was a godsend in her life, too.

She knew it would be a summer of wild and free in so many ways.

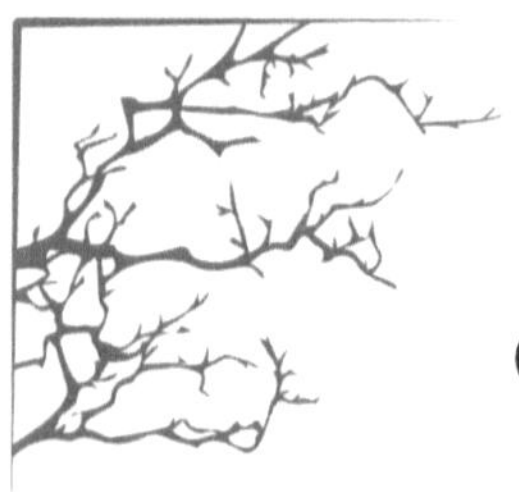

Chapter Twelve

I didn't sleep. Not at all. Because all night, every twig snap, every creek of the house settling, every cricket chirping—I thought it was coming for me.

Visions of those sores, that foul, bubbling skin on that man's naked body—what happened to him? What sort of death did he face in those woods? I can't even imagine. I don't want to imagine. Yet, I have to imagine.

I shudder to remember how the being looked at me as if I were just a plaything for it to chase. Its long, bony fingers wavering in the night air between us as if it were claiming me its own.

I want so badly to tell someone, to get help. I want to spread the word that the woods really aren't safe. But I can't go to them. I can't tell anyone. They'll think I killed that man. They'll think I'm crazy if I tell them what I saw. I've heard the stories of the asylum. I know what happens there. It will not be a reprieve.

~The Journal of H.D. Wards

***

"You look awful," Hazel murmured from across the table, her mouth full of her peanut butter sandwich. The girl swiped at her shiny forehead, her hair matted to it in a characteristically unattractive look. If Hazel thought Mia Rose looked bad, things truly were bad.

Mia Rose itched at her arm, then internally chided herself. It burned when she touched it. She yanked on the sleeves a bit more, staring at her tray of food. She was too nauseous to eat.

"Something wrong?" Hazel prodded. Mia Rose's eyes shot up. She didn't respond, just glaring. Hazel and Mia Rose had a tacit agreement. They ate at the same table at lunch, the one in the back corner. The only table left, in truth, where the two outcasts of the school could eat. Thinking about it, Mia Rose glanced to the front of the cafeteria, where she sat for those few glorious weeks at the end of last school year. How things had changed. How the not-so-mighty had fallen even more.

"Okay, okay. Suit yourself," Hazel murmured when Mia Rose continued to glare. Hazel turned her attention back to her lunch tray and the book in her hand. Mia Rose stared out the window behind the disheveled girl, rubbing her eyes. She really should use this time to fall asleep, she thought. It wouldn't come here—would it? She was admittedly unprepared to make assumptions about the creature.

Just thinking about it, she started to shake, her eyes watering. Weak. She felt so weak. Weaker than she did when her parents studied her with that all-consuming glare. Weaker than she did when she fell to the ground last summer when she heard the news. Weaker than she did before she shared that eye roll with Lilly in that group project.

She suddenly wanted to crawl out of her skin, the memory of her burning flesh making her itch again. An uncontainable whimper escaped her lips as she wildly scratched both of her arms. She was acting like a mad person. Hazel looked up, pale and solemn.

"What did you do to your arm?" she asked. Mia Rose's eyes shot down. Her sleeve had crept up in her frenzy. Just a hint of skin peeked out, but it was enough for the bubbling, decaying boils to make their presence known. The scratches from the creature had turned to pus-filled sacs, pox marks interspersed. Her arm ached and stung, painted red and various colors of death.

"Nothing," she whispered, pulling her sleeve back in place. "Mind your own business." Her voice was gravelly but forceful. She hoped it was enough.

Mia Rose stood to take her tray to the trash. She slung her backpack over her shoulder and slinked away. At least she could be hidden by the bathroom door from prying eyes. Suddenly, it felt like everyone was staring at her, like she had an aura of madness around her. Her arm wounds pulsed as if to confirm her fears.

Her parents had been quiet and cold in the morning, had acted like nothing had happened. She knew better. She heard their whispers, their conniving, plotting discussions. They thought she was on drugs. They were waiting to play their next set of cards. She knew she would be the loser in their game. But when the bell rang for lunch to be over, she emerged from the safety of the bathroom. She sulked down the hallway to her way to sixth-period math class but stopped in the middle when she heard her name on the intercom.

She squeezed her eyes shut, heading to the office to see what new hell awaited her.

Chapter Thirteen

"Miss Ellis, we're just worried about you is all," the pale woman who simultaneously smelled of onions and roses pushed a box of tissues across the desk at her. Mia Rose stared at the inspirational "Keep going" poster behind the redhead's desk, wondering if the woman had spent all those years in college just to learn tissue box pushing techniques.

"I'm fine," Mia Rose muttered, staring straight on at the counselor so as not to arouse suspicion. Mia Rose's mother claimed she could tell when she was lying because of her lack of eye contact. It wouldn't be hard to dupe this woman.

"Look, it's okay to open up. This is a safe space," she said.

Except Mrs. Conney forgot or chose to ignore the fact that Mia Rose had heard those very words before. She'd opened up naively to this woman, thinking she would wave a magic wand and solve her problems. She'd ended up in a car with her parents screaming at her about the whole situation.

She wasn't going to be fooled twice. Besides, what could the mousey woman do? Mia Rose was up against forces of an entirely different variety this time. No amount of counseling could help.

She tapped her sandal on the blue, paper-thin carpet in the office. Mrs. Conney refused to identify the source of the referral, but Mia Rose didn't have to probe to get her answer. Only one person had seen her arm. Only one person could turn her in for potential self-harm. She knew Hazel was trouble, pure and simple. No wonder she didn't have friends if she couldn't mind her own business. No one liked a nark—or a girl with greasy hair, zits, and a tendency for crazy mutterings.

"Look, your parents are on your way. If you won't talk to me, maybe they can at least get you some help. This is serious, Mia Rose. Suicide is nothing to fool around with."

"You called my parents?" Mia Rose shrieked. Her fingers furled into fists. Why couldn't anyone just mind their own business? She didn't need this today. She had enough to worry about.

"I had to call them."

"I'm not suicidal. Please. Can you just send me back to class?"

"Sorry. No can do," Mrs. Conney muttered with that annoying cheerleader smile that seemed wildly inappropriate considering the circumstances. It made Mia Rose uncannily angry.

While the infuriating woman spewed more details about therapy, Mia Rose clenched her jaw, imagining what it would be like if the Flayed One added Mrs. Conney to its list. She would like to see that woman with gashes and boils up and down her arm. Then she would stop smiling. Then she would understand.

This, this thing she was dealing with—it made suicide seem like child's play. Pure child's play. No box of tissues could help, after all, despite Mrs. Conney's insistence that she take one for the road. If only it were so simple.

WITH HER FOREHEAD LEANING on the chilled, grimy glass, Mia Rose peered out the car window as they zoomed towards their house. Both parents had unnecessarily but fiercely come to retrieve her from school. In the parking lot, her mother had demanded to see her arm. Mia Rose had shielded it behind her, not wanting them to see the inexplicable marks and wounds. Her mother took that as the proof she needed. They'd piled into the car.

She rode in the back, an ignored delinquent they wouldn't even look at. She fought the sting of tears as her right hand instinctively stroked her arm.

It had touched her. The thought sent a shudder rippling through her.

"This has got to stop," her mother whispered into the car, breaking the silence. She did not look back at Mia Rose or acknowledge that she was there. The heavy invisibility cloak that oppressed Mia Rose did not lift. "We cannot go there again. We can't. It's too much for this family."

Mia Rose's stomach churned, déjà vu swirling as she remembered what it felt like that first time guidance had called home. That time, though, the marks on her arm were self-made. This time was different. Her parents could not see that, though.

"Sally, stop. This isn't helping," her father jumped in. Mia Rose wasn't sure if he was actually coming to her rescue or if he simply was overwhelmed to the point of exhaustion from all that had transpired. Probably the latter if she had to guess.

"It's not helping? Do you think she is trying to help? Wake up, Luke. She isn't helping herself. She isn't helping us. She made her decisions last summer, and now we're all paying the price. Do you realize I can't even go to work without the sniggers, the stares, the whispers? I've become a fucking outcast because of her. Because of *her*." Her mother's voice was weepy and somber. Mia Rose felt the guilt stab into her gut even though she tried to swallow it down. She wanted to stay numb and stoic. She didn't want her mother's words to pierce her. They did, though. Despite her best efforts, they always did.

An outcast. Mia Rose knew all about that. And she hated how she caused that in her parents. She hated herself for hating that. She hated everything.

Maybe it would be better for everyone if it ended me, she thought as her parents bickered on as if she had already left. Maybe without her, they would return to a life of quiet. They would go back to their pot roast on Mondays and light banter about the game show on television. Her mother would return to running the church bake sales while her father effortlessly read the newspaper, golfed on Fridays, and just sat in the monotony of a life familiar.

Maybe she shouldn't wait for the creature—

Her grandmother's face came to mind, though. The sweet woman who had always accepted her, who had been a warm home for her when her own house had turned cold. Mia Rose couldn't just leave her. Not after all she'd done for her. She pictured her grandmother in her dying days staring out into the abyss of the forest, waiting for a granddaughter to return who was long gone. If her grandmother could be brave, she would have to be as well. She couldn't leave, no matter what.

Her focus tuned back to the front seat conversation that was about her but not for her.

The word asylum rang out in the air, like a piece of small-talk or a discussion of dinner foods. Their casual attitude toward the conversation chilled Mia Rose. Perhaps this was their perfect excuse, the necessary reason to send her away, to make her someone else's problem. Mia Rose thought about the stories she'd heard, about the sight of that macabre building in the middle of a forest island. What was worse—to be pursued by a monster, or to be forgotten at the hands of monsters in human form? She chilled, remembering the threat from last year. She'd thought it was an empty scare tactic to force her into submission and obedience. It had worked then. It was working now. But she was different than the girl of last summer. She had to learn to be different.

Decisions had wrecked her life. All of the decisions leading up to that fateful moment. The decision right now to stay. The decision to go back into those woods. Her life was a fleeting line of choices that led her down her path. It was a dark, enigmatic path full of pain, but at least it was hers. Freedom, she knew, was the most important thing, more important than safety or life.

Thus, she made the decision right there. She would not let that happen. She would do what she had to do. She would not let them commit her to the asylum in the forest, something potentially even more terrifying than the beast who had marred her arm.

A thought struck her as an annoyingly jovial song blared on the radio, her father cranking the dial presumably to turn out her mother's yapping—she could at least be happy for that. The thought was a minuscule ant crawling up her arm, up her shoulder, into her ear. She wanted to squeeze it with a pair of pointy tweezers. She ached to pluck it from her skin and burn it. Still, its legs kept prickling at her skin, tickling her jaw.

What if it *was* madness taking over?

Perhaps grief coupled with stress coupled with her morose imagination was finally creating a toxic concoction, a stew of fear. At the thought, though, her fingers automatically squeezed her burning arm. She winced in pain, but at least she knew. Anytime she thought it wasn't real, she had proof right there. Was that why it did it, why it left its mark? Least a victim talk down the fear?

They rounded the familiar bend, and the car crunched onto the gravel road that twisted toward their house. Her eyes studied the tree line, a gloom permeating the woods that incited dread to the onlooker. Her parents continued bickering, not even looking.

But Mia Rose was looking, staring, studying. She squeezed her arm so tightly that a whimper escaped her lips. Her parents were so entranced by their argument, they didn't notice.

It was only for a moment, the car speeding on down the road. She turned her head to look at it for as long as possible, drawn to it like one is drawn to a car accident or drawn to the sky when it is said to be falling. She could not look away.

When they had passed it, the stalk-still body hovered between two trees. To one not trained to spot it, The Flayed One would blend in with the darkness. For Mia Rose, though, already disposed to see nothing but it, her eyes caught sight of it immediately. Its arm was outstretched, its tendril pointing toward her with the razor-sharp claw. At the memory of it, her arm burned and grew hot. The mark of the creature. The mark of her death.

The car came to a stop. Mia Rose anxiously stared at the woods.

"Mia Rose, hello? What's wrong with you?"

She snapped back to attention. Her mother was outside of the car, screaming at her to get out. She stared at the woman who had become more adversary than family, but she felt numb. It did not matter anymore. Nothing mattered anymore.

The dread spread like a wicked shame, like a poisoned fruit in her blood.

She looked over her shoulder as she walked toward the house. There was nothing.

Silence, darkness, and trees that cloaked the unknown that had become known to her.

How long would she be able to avoid sleep?

Chapter Fourteen

It comes at night. When you're trying to drift off and forget it even exists, it comes along and haunts your waking nightmares. I tried to lay down last night and forget about it. I attempted to talk myself out of its existence. Exhaustion overwhelmed all of my senses. I wanted to slip into oblivion like I did before I saw it. I convinced myself for a brief moment that there had to be an explanation for it all. I'd just been spooked in the forest, and my imagination had run wild. The stories of my youth plagued my weary mind and played tricks on me. I hadn't seen anything at all.

But the body—the rotting flesh. The decaying corpse. I tried to shove that out of my mind. Waves of weariness slammed into my body and rippled through my core. My bones begged to sleep, to rest, to be at peace.

I sank into my bed, tension gripping every muscle in my body. I coaxed my eyes into shutting and my mind into taking me away to that dream world where the horrors of reality can be still.

Before I could drift away, though, on a cloud of unconsciousness, it came.

At first, I thought the tree outside my room tapped on the window, its branches scratching against the filmy glass. My eyes squeezed shut, I told myself the wind was blowing it into the glass like it sometimes did, creating shadows on the wall from the cast of the moonlight that used to scare me as a child. The tapping grew louder, though, and my stomach sank.

I bolted up and looked out the window. The tree stood stoic, unwavering. No wind rattled its branches. I held my breath.

And when the tapping turned to a frenetic scratching, my heart chilled. I inched against the headboard of my bed, my eyes not wanting to see but also needing to see. The scratching returned to tapping.

Rap. Rap. Tap.

Tap. Tap. Rap.

Screech. Screech tap tap.

It was as if a morse code were playing out on the grimy window.

I inched forward, telling myself it was nothing. A raccoon. A bear. Something of that variety. My desperate mind searched for an antidote to the terror usurping my entire being.

Deep down, though, I knew. The putrid smell wafting in told me all I needed to know. I crept forward in the blackness of my room, my feet edging along the carpet even though they wanted nothing more than to dash away. I pushed onward, the short distance between my bed and the window an ocean of horrors.

When I got to the window sill, my heart stopped. My fingers shook and my chest stung.

There it stood, peering at me with an unshattered confidence. It knew I would come. It had just been waiting.

~The Journal of H.D. Wards

***

They didn't berate her when they got home as she assumed they would. Instead, they let her sulk away to her room, and they separated themselves into the living area. Her versus them, as it had become. She heard raised whispers echoing and knew they were about her. But they did not have it out or sit her down for a deep discussion about her wellbeing like they had before. Maybe they had given up on her. Maybe she had, too. After time passed, she emerged from her room to find them watching television together.

"There's some dinner in the fridge," her mother said without taking her gaze away from the competition show they were watching.

Mia Rose glanced out the window, dread usurping her as she expected to see it. Nonetheless, there was nothing but the grayish light of dusk. She should stay home, the thought of it lurking about making her want to entomb herself in the basement forever. Still, glancing at the cold boredom in the living room, the judgmental tension floating about, she knew she had to take the risk.

"I'm going to see Grandma," she announced, heading to the door before she lost her nerve or her freedom.

"Be back by dark," her father demanded.

"I will," she assured. And she knew she would.

Walking out the door, she shuddered as her eyes frenetically scanned the trees, looking for a terrifying claw, the towering being seeking to inflict hell upon her. She touched her arm, wincing at the stinging sensation.

She could run away, be gone from this place for good. She could walk straight to town, to the bus stop, to a new life that would be uncertain but certainly couldn't be any worse. Would it follow her if she left? H.D. hadn't tried, at least from what she knew. She had no way of knowing for sure. Her feet following the well-trodden path, she marched on, knowing that despite her reverent daydreams of new starts, she couldn't leave. She couldn't abandon the one person who had devoted her life to her, had shown her unconditional love.

She wanted to see her because her grandmother was a natural comfort in a darkened world. Deep down, though, Mia Rose also knew her other reason for the visit.

It would come back.

And eventually, it would come for its final time. There would be no surviving it. Whether she died here or in a town she didn't know the name of, there would be no escaping it. She didn't even need the words of a frenetic boy to know that. Sometimes you just had to accept your fate.

Why was it so hard, then, to accept what had happened last summer? Why couldn't she chalk that up to fate? She knew why. The guilt illuminated the why.

Her days numbered, she marched on in the fading sun to see the woman who meant so much—and to perhaps say the tacit goodbye they'd both been dreading for months. It was just they both never expected it would be Mia Rose who would be the first to go.

SHE PICKED AT THE FUZZ ball on the couch as Edmund slept on her feet. Her grandmother turned off the competition show, the same one her parents were watching at home.

"Talk to me, Dear," her grandmother croaked, her voice frail today.

"Grandma, we've *been* talking," Mia Rose said gently. Edmund stirred on the floor.

"But you haven't really been talking. You've been talking about the weather and the television show but not what's actually on your mind."

That was Grandma. She could always see through to the truth.

Her Grandma scooted closer on the couch, groaning slightly as she did. The pain was getting worse now. Her pallor was grayer than the rubbery meat the cafeteria served or a wisp of fog. Mia Rose's heart constricted a bit more.

"I know you still blame yourself," her grandma began, quietly. "You shouldn't. Things are often out of our control. I know it doesn't make the pain go away. But we all lose things, Mia Rose. We lose people. We get our hearts broken. We have to find a way to go on, though."

Mia Rose had never uttered words to her grandma about that horrid day last summer. She hadn't revealed her heart or explained it all through her sobs. She didn't need to. Her grandma knew. She just knew, in ways her parents never could.

Mia Rose's mind floundered for an escape from the stabbing memories. The throbbing pain of her arm drew her attention back to the present troubles. She pulled her sleeve down a bit more as she thought about the name Dorothy Mae in the journal. The question lingered, dancing on her tongue and wanting to be asked. She bit her lip, not ready to confide, to lay her troubles on the already suffering woman. It had to be her. She had to know H.D. How much more did her grandma know? She wanted to ask, wanted to expose all her secrets. But her grandmother coughed, reaching for her hankie to wipe away the spittle mixed with the tinge of blood that was common now—and also a clear reminder of what was to come. Soon.

Mia Rose couldn't worry her like that. She couldn't. No matter how badly she needed answers, she wouldn't have her grandmother's final days scarred with worry for her, a concern that would do no good.

"How do you say goodbye when you never got the chance?" Mia Rose asked instead, her voice a whispered prayer.

Her grandmother's soft eyes seemed to look beyond to a place Mia Rose did not know or could not know—yet somehow knew entirely.

"I don't think you ever do, Dear. You just learn to live with the questions."

The sun was quickly fading now. It was time to return home, to the thin veil of safety her house could offer against the great unknown of the wilderness. She thought about staying but did not want to risk it. She didn't want her grandmother to bear witness to the beast—for if her grandmother was Dorothy Mae from the journal, the beast had let her live. Mia Rose wouldn't risk that now for her selfish quest for answers and safety.

She didn't say goodbye. She left the questions to linger. She softly kissed her grandmother's cheek, told her she loved her and closed the door behind her as she faced the unremitting blackness about to settle over them all.

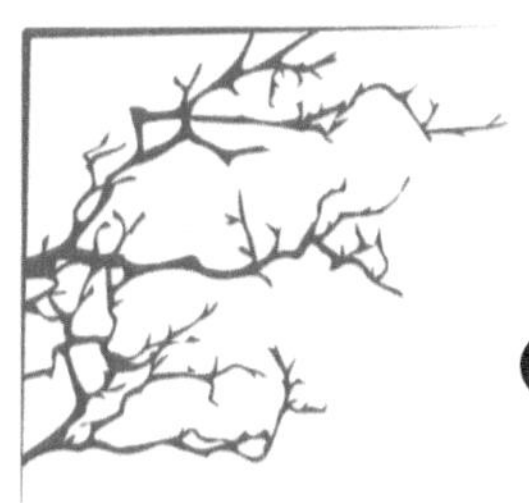

Chapter Fifteen

"She's been crazy since last year. Since the whole situation. When you're that age, you get wrapped up in feelings anyway and—"

The voice of her father had been a muffled whisper echoing through the kitchen. She'd stood on the porch, leaning on the front door long enough to hear the words.

Crazy. They thought she was crazy. Perhaps she was. She threw open the door, not wanting to hear their discounting admonishments or their attempts to scar what memories she had left of her.

"Oh, you're home. How was Grandma?" her mother asked, her dad reddening a bit at being caught mid-rant about her. Mia Rose once would have argued with them, would have ranted and raged about them talking about her like that. Now, she just stood complacently.

"You'd know if you took the time to visit her more," Mia Rose spewed, knowing the words would be a bloody stab in her mother's already cold, splintered heart.

"Get to your room," her mother bellowed. Mia Rose was all too happy to comply.

But once in her room, she rocked on her bed thinking about the inevitability of it all. Was that how she felt, alone in those woods, knowing what was to come yet not knowing at all?

Tears rolled down her cheeks. It would be painful. She knew it would be painful. But maybe it was pain that allowed peace to come. She would have to hope.

Night settled over them. The house grew quiet. She sat and listened to the wind fluttering outside. She thought she could hear a moan, a sigh in the distance as if Mother Earth herself were tense about the battle to come.

She wrapped her blanket around her shoulders covering her chest. She felt for the knife she'd carefully planted under her pillow. It was still there. They hadn't upturned her room—yet. A small relief in a field of sorrow. What little comfort, though, the blade was against the blades of the creature, against its wily strength, its stealthy movements.

If it wanted her—it would have her. It was a truth that radiated from her core, yet she fought its veracity all the same. The minutes ticked by. The hours crawled on. Her eyes drooped heavily but she fought for the light of the day.

Her gaze was planted on the windowpanes, studying every crevice, every crack, every bit of peeling, white paint.

Dawn was approaching when it finally came. When its claws rapped on the glass. When its icy black holes for eyes glared into her room, its melting face pressed against the dirty window. The smell and the scream simultaneously swamped her senses again. She squeezed her eyes shut, willing it away. Praying it away. She opened them again. It stood still, both hands pressed against the glass as if she were an animal in a zoo exhibit as if she were a lobster in a tank waiting to be plucked out and tossed into the boiling pot.

Why didn't it just kill her? Why? She wanted to thrust open the window and let it do its job, let it take her from the suffering of the when and why and how. The sight of its claws, the sting of her arm from its touch stopped her. She'd never been a martyr.

Please, make it stop, she begged a merciless universe. The sound carried on, the pain rattling through her charred arm and agitating the burning sensation. She pulled back a sleeve and watched as the skin seemed to melt a bit more, as the boils leached and blackened.

And then, just as quickly as it had started, it all stopped. The sound faded into silence, which was somehow more bone-chilling than the rattling noise. She caught her breath, her voice aching even though she did not bother to scream. Who would she beckon forth anyway? Who would come to her aid? It would just add to their madness theory, and the asylum was not the retreat she sought. Her hands shook with the need to do something, with the desperation to be believed.

She stumbled to her writing desk. It would give her a chance to keep watch. It could come back, after all. It would always come back. Her hands quaked as she grabbed for a piece of paper, a pencil.

If she was good at art, she would've sketched it. But she never had been. So instead, she started writing the phrase most forward in her mind.

You will not be saved.

You will not be saved.

YOU will not be saved.

Morning came. Her paper was filled. She lived to see the dawn, but she didn't know if her heart was filled with gratitude for her breath or envy for those it could no longer come back for.

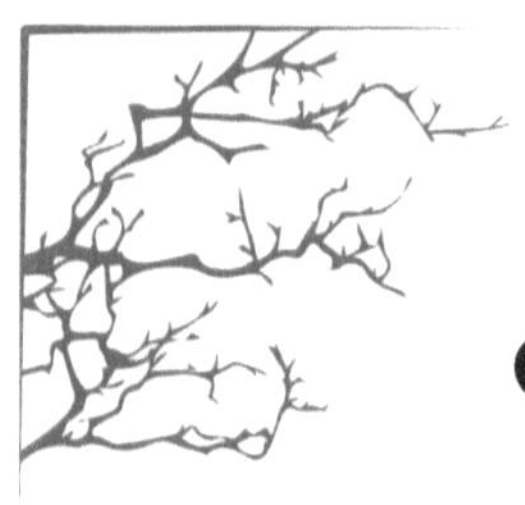

Chapter Sixteen

*M*ia Rose opened the door, telling herself to contain her beaming smile. She'd put on her yellow dress at her mother's insistence, but Lilly wore her signature ripped jeans, a T-shirt, and a black leather jacket. Mia Rose wished she hadn't listened to her mother's lecture about being a proper host.

"Hey," Mia Rose offered, trying to assuage the bubbling nerves in her chest.

"Hey," Lilly replied, giving a little wave.

It had been Mia Rose's mother's idea. She'd asked who Mia Rose had been spending so much time with, and when she had told her, Mother insisted she needed to meet her.

"She's just a friend, Mother. I don't see why you need to go to all the trouble of meeting her."

"You're spending time with her. I want to know more about her. Nothing wrong with a mother keeping her eye on her impressionable daughter's reputation." She's said the words over her cup of tea, pinkie out as if she were the Queen of England approving her son's suitor. Mia Rose had rolled her eyes, but as the conversation ensued, she'd finally agreed to invite Lilly over to shut her mother up.

In truth, she was terrified. Lilly was not the kind of girl Mother approved of. She'd gotten the sense from their conversations that Lilly's home was not one where she'd ever be invited for a sit-down dinner. And from what she'd learned about her dad—

Mother would never want her daughter hanging out with someone like that. But Mia Rose thought that maybe if she had her over for dinner, they could change her mother's mind.

After calm pleasantries, her mother led them to the table where she'd set out the pot roast like a perfect 1950's housewife. Mia Rose fought the urge to roll her eyes at her mother's insistence of saying grace—always displaying the religious views on the forefront. The crucifix her mother wore around her neck was a perfectly pious backdrop to the holy words she uttered in a solemn tone.

After the religious fervor of the family had been prominently showcased, they started to eat. The conversation was going fine. Her father asked Lilly about her post-high school plans. They talked about classic cars, something Lilly was into. The pot roast was passed around, and Mia Rose took a deep breath.

But then her mother started being—her mother. Nagging Mia Rose to sit up straight. Harassing her about her low math grade. Pointing out the hair growing on her chin that needed keeping up with. Mia Rose was mortified. Her mother was pleased.

"Well, Mia Rose. You're at that time in your life when you need to take care of yourself. Men won't just come calling for no reason, you know. And we all know you're not smart enough to go into the career world on your own. You're going to need some support."

Her mother laughed as if she was exceedingly proud of herself. Mia Rose's face and heart stung. She'd never been the best at school, the best at anything really. She looked down at her plate, shoving food around as she remembered how inadequate even her own family felt she was. Suddenly, the perfect bubble that had been the summer with Lilly burst into a thousand pieces.

"Maybe she doesn't want a man to save her. You know? It's modern times, Ms. Ellis. Not everyone needs a man. There are other paths to choose." And at that, Lily winked at her mother, a cocky wink that suggested she knew exactly what she was doing. Mia Rose smirked. Her mother raged. One did not challenge Sally Ellis without waging war. One did not make her feel inferior.

"Get the hell out," her mother bellowed, tossing down the cloth napkin she'd gotten out just for the occasion. A part of Mia Rose was glad to see the true side of the holier-than-thou woman emerge, the side she'd been privy to all those years. Behind the perfect apple pies and prayerful Sundays was a narcissistic woman who hungered for power at all costs. "Everyone said you were a good for nothing girl. Now I know why. I won't have you disrespecting me in my own house."

"Mother," Mia Rose murmured. Her mother had gone too far dragging Lilly into it. She wanted to strike the woman down, to run out the door and never come back. But Lilly was already on her feet, wily confidence in the girl that was certainly a match for her elder.

"It would be my pleasure to leave. Thank you so much for the titillating conversation."

Mia Rose tried to stop her, but Lilly smiled at her. "It's okay. The pleasure of being our age is that we get the chance to grow up to be something better than our parents. Looks like we both have pretty good chances of that."

And then, she was gone, out the door faster than a fly but with a confident stride that told everyone to make no mistake—she was not ashamed. Mia Rose stood stunned and mortified in the wake of her presence. She turned to her mother, enraged.

"How could you? How could you be so rude? She's my friend."

"And I'm your mother. I know what girls like her are all about. You don't need to get wrapped up in her scene."

Mia Rose's dad cleared his throat and then thought better of saying anything, the glare from his wife silencing him. He started moving dishes off the table, meandering into the kitchen and not coming back. The two women stood in an icy staring contest, both challenging each other wordlessly.

The self-proclaimed champion broke the silence.

"You are to never see that awful girl again. You aren't a child, Mia Rose. Your reputation matters. I will not have you spending time with the child of the town drunk who also happens to be a smart-mouthed brat."

"I thought you wanted to get to know her," Mia Rose argued, exasperated.

"It's a small town, and you're our only daughter. Do you think I don't know things? Do you think I don't do my research?"

"So what, this was a goddamn setup? So you could get rid of her?"

"This was me doing my motherly duties and checking out the situation. Be glad I did that. I gave her a chance, but she's exactly what they say she is. Rude and smug. An idiot, in truth."

"But—"

"I'm the adult here, in case you've forgotten. Me. So until you're out of here doing who knows what on your own, it's my rules. My rules. You will not see her again."

Her mother had sealed it with those words, for if anyone knows anything about teenagers, they know this—the forbidden is a delectable treasure sought after at all costs.

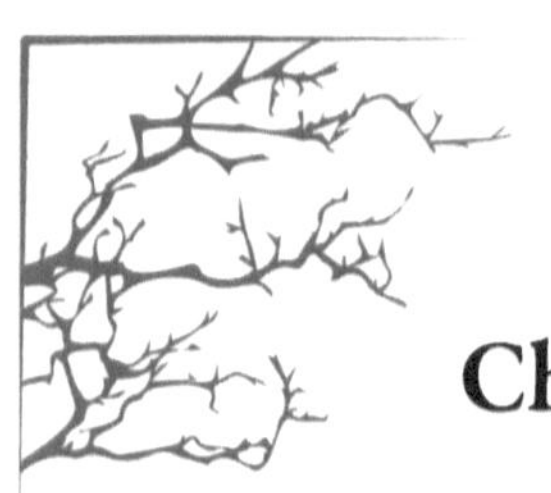

Chapter Seventeen

I'm doing something rash, something I never thought I'd do—going to the library in town. Books have never kept me company, but today is different. I need to sort this out, and I don't know where else to start. I'm going to see what articles, what books I can find. There has to be a record of that thing in the woods. I can't be the only one who has seen it. There has to be an answer.

I DON'T KNOW HOW WE ever thought the stories were just legends.

Fifty-two.

Fifty-two missing in the past few decades with no explanations. Some from Cedarcrest, some from Redwood. Some from nearby towns. Fifty-two that we know of who went into the woods and never came out or just vanished near the edges of both towns. Some were asylum patients who were reported. Some were small children, a few hikers. Many, many teenagers who were said to have just vanished, perhaps who ran away.

Abigail Woodward, fifteen. 1955. She lived in Redwood and was last seen walking with a hood up near the asylum. She was never found.

John Benson. Five. 1951. He got away from his parents during a party at a friend's house near the edge of Oakwood. He was never found and presumed missing in the forest or kidnapped.

Emily Cartright. 1960. Escaped from Redwood Asylum. Entire chunks of her red curls were found scattered a mile out from the asylum, but she was never recovered.

Edward Cartright. 1960. Emily's husband went looking for her and never returned from the woods. A search team returned with his gold watch with his initials, but despite the family's mass of wealth and search efforts, he was never recovered.

Jonathan Eberhart. 16. Disappeared in 1965 from his porch in Cedarcrest. His parents said he was there and then just gone. He'd been complaining of night terrors. The police determined him to be a runaway.

Ethan Allison. 1971. He was a hitchhiker who was spotted in town. He checked into the motel in Cedarcrest and then never came back. His parents came looking for him, claiming he was going into the Redwood forest to investigate after talking to a friend. He never came out.

So many went into those woods or near them. So many never returned. I chill at the thought that the woods by my house are a glorified, open hour cemetery, the being a harbinger of death and a mortician all the same.

Stories of searches scanning through the woods, yet only two bodies were ever found back in the late 1940s. The newspaper article from that period notes the bodies were in disarray, but what does that mean?

***

550503363411 End.

Answers. Sitting in the uncomfortable library chair, she knew that the one thing she needed to survive, if she were to survive at all, would be answers. But as she typed the mysterious number from the last page of H.D. Wards' journal into the search engine, Mia Rose hoped to scroll through results. She hoped the answer would be there on her screen. Instead, the search engine returned exactly zero results.

No results at all. How could that be? It irked her to the core thinking about what the number was. A code of some sort? For what? The number had flashed in her mind over and over, a riddle that probably meant nothing but perhaps meant everything. Why did he end with that number? Was he truly just mad?

She stared into space, the creature's image flashing in her mind's eye as she shuddered. The library was like a sauna, the elderly librarian having the heat blasting even though it was a perfectly warm day. Nevertheless, goosebumps prickled on Mia Rose's arms, causing her wounds to burn. She decided on a different tactic, typing in "The Flayed One" to the search box.

She'd done this already, and the results were familiar. Xipe Totec showed up, a fertility god of the Aztecs. But it was not her Flayed One, not the monster that wormed its way through her waking dreams. Of the beast that toyed with her, there was nothing. All she had to verify her sanity was the lost journal of a boy who seemingly vanished into thin air and the memories of what she saw. She was alone, all alone. Vomit rose in her gut.

She wished it were like the movies. She longed to be a wise, detective-like girl who would find the answers on the computer and chase the monster down. She wished she were a different girl altogether, born into a different time and place where life wasn't so difficult or dull or just plain heavy. But wishes belonged on birthday candles of little girls, not on almost women who knew how evil the world was.

Lost in a cloak of frustration, she aimlessly scrolled, glancing up to give her stinging eyes a break and to soothe the tension headache building. Across from her, a woman sat at the computer, her blonde hair in a ponytail. Mia Rose glanced at her over the top of her desktop, noting the bags under her eyes and the bloodshot quality, the pale grayness of her. She clacked on the keys rabidly, her desperation for answers to whatever she was researching blatant. Mia Rose pounded on her keyboard, an urge to blurt out a question strengthening: *Have you seen anything in the Redwood Forest?* It seemed preposterous, but somehow, the way the blonde carried herself, the despondent look in her eyes—it seemed to cry out to Mia Rose, to mark a sense of comradery in suffering between them. Still, Mia Rose knew some secrets needed to be guarded. She knew that as much as the question, the words about whether the frazzled blonde had seen the creature danced on her tongue, she had to swallow the phrase down. She was alone in it, just as the woman was alone in whatever mystery she was in search of.

She rose from her computer to leave, feeling more defeated than before.

She didn't know why, but she looked at the woman, offered a weak smile, and said, "Good luck."

The woman didn't respond, lost in her own world that Mia Rose was privy to despite her best efforts.

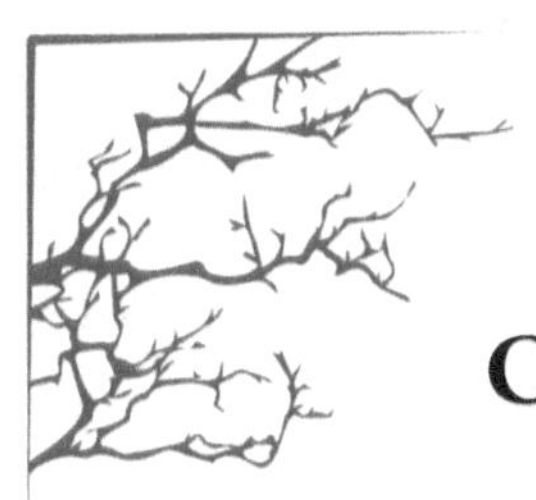

Chapter Eighteen

Not all the days at their forest refuge were peaceful days to remember. One in particular haunted Mia Rose long after the dust had cleared and she understood the truth—Lilly was a complicated girl. She'd thought she knew her that summer, knew her better than anyone. She knew that was why her mother was so adamant she didn't see the girl. She knew Lilly was haunted by a reality that was probably much murkier than even the rumors let on. But later, as she thought over the moments they had shared, the truth resurrected. The girl was an enigma, both in life and in death.

They were sitting by the tree stump, a few keychains added to the collection. Lilly picked at the grass, her usually bubbly personality settled, calm, willful, as she stared into the misty forest.

"I need to leave this place, Mi. I need to get out."

Mia Rose smiled at the pet name she'd given her just the other day. But as the words' meaning sank in, panic ruffled her.

"What do you mean?"

Lilly sighed, picking at the blade of grass, eventually tucking it between two carefully placed thumbs to create the makeshift whistle she often did.

"I can't do it much longer. This place. That house. It's wearing on me. It's changing me. I don't want it to change me."

Mia Rose brushed a piece of Lilly's hair back. She'd seen the bruises once when they'd gone swimming in the creek at the start of summer. They'd trailed down her back, on her chest. Mia Rose's questioning eyes had then been met with a guarded stare and eventually the truth—a truth that made Mia Rose's skin burn.

"I know. Soon. You'll be out of that place soon."

Tears welled in Lilly's eyes as she pulled her knees in. "I don't know. I don't know how long I can hang on. I don't even know if there's anything else out there for me."

Mia Rose scooched closer, leaning her head on the vulnerable redhead's shoulder. She gently placed her hand in the girl's lap, entwining her fingers around hers.

"We'll runaway together. As soon as the time is right. We'll leave this place behind. Your mother and disgusting Rick won't be able to touch you anymore. I promise. Just be patient a little while longer."

Lilly turned to look into her eyes, and Mia Rose saw comfort there, understanding. She knew the rumors were flying. She worried what her parents would say—old-school, conservative to the core. They flipped the channel as soon as two guys were kissing on a sitcom. What would they say? She buried the deep-seated fear from her childhood, the whispers that echoed.

You're not good enough.

You're a disappointment.

You have disgraced your family.

Before, those phrases stirred when she got in trouble at school or when her grades weren't good enough. Now, the voice broadcasted in her head said her feelings were wrong, that they'd never accept this embarrassment.

Girls grew up to be married women. She was to grow up and marry a respectable boy, have children, a house. Her mother already had the China set put away for her.

But as Lilly nuzzled into her, the girl who had started as a friend and turned to something else quickly, Mia Rose told herself none of that mattered. She'd found the one who understood her. It all made sense now. Did things like social norms and constructs matter when her heart was so full?

"I would die without you, Mia Rose. I'm so glad we were in that group together. You're my everything now. My everything."

Her fingers curled tighter around hers, and in the middle of their secret sanctuary, two broken, fearful girls comforted each other as their hearts grew closer. No one was there to witness it except the forest and the creatures inside of it.

No one had to know, *Mia Rose reminded herself as she sat down across from her parents a few hours later for dinner.*

No one would know until the time was right. And then, it wouldn't matter at all.

Chapter Nineteen

Sleep was a desperate craving Mia Rose could not quench at home. Thus, her already slipping grades started to fall even more as she struggled to keep her eyes open in class. Even when she drifted into the dreamland inspired by Algebraic equations and Mr. Hinton's monotone voice, sleep was a fitful rage tarnished by nightmares of it.

It haunted her nights. It plagued her dreams. It wisped about in her mind even in the broad daylight. Her hands shook constantly, and her arm screamed out in agony.

It needed to end. She wanted it to end. But she also wasn't ready.

Mia Rose jumped, a tapping near her ear startling her. A scream came out of her lips, and the classroom burst into laughter. She put a hand to her heart as she realized it wasn't the creature—just an annoying math teacher. He towered over her, and she wiped the groggy sleep from her eyes. How long had she been out? What had she missed?

"Ms. Ellis, that is quite enough. If you're so bored, why don't you leave?"

"I'm sorry."

"Get out. Sorry doesn't cut it."

Mia Rose sighed. If only he knew—no. Even a creature spawned from hell wouldn't be an acceptable excuse for the stick-in-the-mud teacher. She sighed, gathered her bag and books, and sulked out of the classroom, both mortified and relieved. She beelined for the bathroom, needing some cold water and perspective that only a high school mirror can provide.

She was relieved to find the bathroom empty, the puke green tiles her only company. She studied herself in the mirror. She'd popped a bright blue headband on today to take attention away from her frizzy hair and sullen skin. It wasn't helping, though.

She leaned closer to the makeup-covered mirror. She was examining the zit on her face when she saw a flash of something in the mirror. She turned around.

Nothing. No one. Emptiness.

She shook her head at her paranoia incited by weariness. She turned on the tap and splashed some cold water on her face, not caring if it smeared the little mascara she'd managed to put on. Eyes closed and water splashing on her face, she felt something touch her back. She froze, eyes still closed, afraid to even breathe as her blood chilled. She didn't dare move a muscle, didn't even blink as her whole body tensed.

All was quiet.

She must have imagined it.

She knew she hadn't.

Please, please let her have imagined it.

Slowly, she peeled open her eyes, her face dripping with water.

And then, the scream came out, a moaning train whistle in the distance, an agonizing pierce louder than the bell.

She ran for the door, still screaming and wondering one word over and over:

How? How? How?

She collided into a solid body at the door, and suddenly, she was on the ground.

"WHAT A FREAK," A VOICE murmured above her.

"Is she okay?"

"Should we get the nurse?"

Panicked female voices danced around her as she opened her eyes, staring up at long hair and questioning faces.

Her immediate thought was to sit up and look for it. The creature. She couldn't see past the circle of pink, though. She scrambled to her feet, body aching and chest heaving. Her hands still trembled, and her heart felt as if it had stopped altogether.

"Excuse me," Mia Rose blurted out, shoving past them, needing nothing more than air and space and freedom.

"What a psycho," a voice announced as the bathroom door swung open and Mia Rose escaped.

She did not stop to argue or to question anyone. She did not ask for permission. She brushed by the busy hallways and the glowering students. She made it to the front door, walked out, and didn't look back.

There would be hell to pay for this when her parents found out. But there was hell anyway, as she'd come to learn.

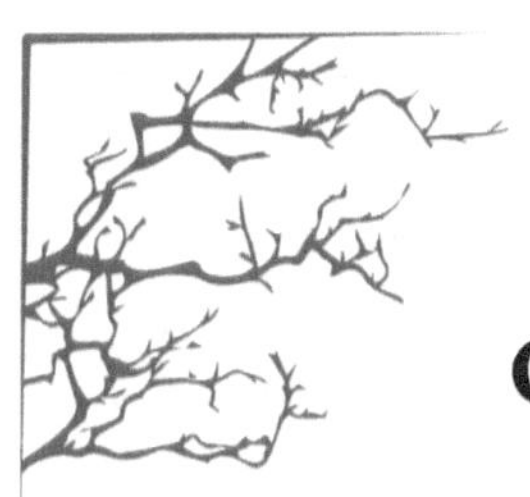

Chapter Twenty

The days passed in monotonous, weary succession. Fatigue debilitated her. She could not sleep, yet she could not bear the waking hours, either.

It had not come since the school bathroom incident which was—what? Two? Three days ago? Time no longer meant anything. For she knew, if not this minute, then the next. If not today, then tomorrow. Its lurking body, its razor-sharp nails would return. And then, all would be over. Sometimes, in the middle of the excessive, debilitating fatigue, it seemed like it would be a treasure to rest her eyes for the final time.

She sat at the table, thinking about her life and all that had transpired when her parents sat down across from her. They had not said more to her about all that had transpired, had not sought to punish her more than grounding her. They also, though, had not tried to find her help—no therapists, no doctors, no mentions of the asylum. They seemed to be taking the side of letting her keep a low profile, most likely to keep the embarrassment down. It had become overabundantly apparent that her wellbeing was not their utmost concern—and never was. It was a blessing in some ways to not have to put mental faculties towards covering up her issues with them. It was also the curse of being unloved, uncared for, unsupported.

"Your father and I are leaving tonight, Mia Rose. Your Great Uncle Mike has passed away. There's food in the fridge. We'll be back late tomorrow." Her mother uttered the sentences robotically as if she were leaving a message on a doctor's answering machine. There was no emotion, no extension of care for her only daughter. The cold, callousness of it all stung.

"What?" she asked, the first sense of care she'd expressed in days bubbling up. She did not remember Great Uncle Mike, had no wasteland of memories to trudge through. Her vehement disapproval, though, came from a place of fear and disbelief.

Had they given up on her so much now that they dared leave her alone? There had been the self-harm scares and talks about her going crazy. They had been talking about asylums and bad behavior and, of course, she was grounded now that she'd left school. But the fact they were willing to give all of that up to go to a funeral, alone—why? Did they dislike her so much? Did they hope she would disappear? It was incredulous to even believe—that they had slipped so far out of sync as a family, they were completely apathetic to it all.

"I'll go with you," she added in desperation, the thought of being alone in the house that night enough to make her swallow her pride.

"You'll do no such thing," her mother ordered quietly, stoically. "It's best you stay here."

"Why?" she whispered, and for a moment, she thought she detected that maternal instinct, that unconditional love that bubbles in even the most disgusted women.

"Because we don't want the family knowing of your—condition." Her mother was blunt but quiet, as if the softness of her voice would ease the blow.

"What condition?"

"Mia Rose, we know a lot is going on for you. We know. We'll talk about it some other time. I can't deal with it all right now, with everything. I need to be there for dad. When we get back, we will handle everything. Sit down, have a real conversation about what our course of action will be. Please just try to stay out of trouble for a day or two." The woman icily got up from the table and crossed the kitchen. Case closed. A daughter written off.

"Mom, please," Mia Rose begged. "I cannot stay here alone. It's not safe."

Her mother turned. "You're not. You'll stay with Grandma. You can head over there later."

Mia Rose's chest constricted. Grandma. Her dear Grandma, the poor victim by association in this disaster.

Her parents left an hour later, a succinct and effortless goodbye. She headed to her room to think it over, to make a plan—but the thing with plans was you had to have the energy and the resources to make them. She was lost, a directionless boat in a dark, dark sea. Her grandmother would go down with the ship.

She sat at her desk and pulled open her laptop. She was feeling nostalgic, wistful even. Life had never been perfect, but it had never been this bad, either. She scrolled through the files, watching videos that made her eyes well up. A life well-lived? A life well-lived.

And then, it was there, standing in the rays of the sun, watching her with hunger.

A life lived.

Chapter Twenty-One

Mia Rose dashed to the front door to make sure it was bolted tightly. Hands shaking, she threw the lock so violently, her hand ached. She told herself to stay calm, to breathe, that it was outside, a fact that could change. Moving swiftly to the kitchen, she grabbed for the chef's knife her dad used on weekends when he played Gordon Ramsay. Now, the knife was her sense of relief, her promise of safety. She clung to it like the lifeblood it potentially was.

She stood stone still, her back against the refrigerator. She didn't want it to surprise her.

The only sound filling the house was her breathing. She inhaled, exhaled. Terror seized her ability to think. She should call her parents. She should call for help. But what help would they offer? They would simply believe her to be mad, and then she would find herself trapped in a newfound hell. She would have to brave up, man up, as H.D. Wards' journal had said. She shivered to think about how it all probably turned out for him.

Her fingers curled around the knife, she listened for the sound of breaking glass, of opening doors. Nothing. After a long moment, she crept forward into the darkened kitchen, searching for the courage to peer out the window. She wanted it to be over yet also didn't. She wasn't ready to face the pain she knew would be hers if it came again. Her arm, putrid and scorched, was proof of its powers. She didn't want to explore its abilities any more thoroughly.

Inch by inch, her feet moved toward the kitchen window. She steadied her breath, told herself to stay calm. At the window, she gazed out, holding her breath and . . .

Nothing. Silence. Stone-still trees. The shimmering grass of the backyard. Nothing.

But the hint of the smell wafted in, wrapping around her nose, her body, her hair. It was just a hint, but it was still pungent enough to make her gag. Her body quivered in repulsion. She knew what was to come.

Before she could make it back the hallway to her bedroom where she'd left her phone, there was fiddling at the lock on the front door. Rattling metal startled her. She squeezed the knife even tighter, the blood running out of her hand.

The jiggling of the doorknob and violent scratching caused her to back up. It was hellbent on getting in. She reassured herself that the door was heavy, that the lock was solid. But the lock had been solid all those other nights, too. It rattled and scratched, its nails grating on the wood. Her feet scurried across the floor, backing up toward the hallway. It wouldn't get in, she lied to herself. She was safe inside. She was safe. It wouldn't get—

The door flung open, and silhouetted by the hazy moon, it posed in the threshold. Its slender, gargantuan body upright in the door, her eyes were glued to the fiendish majesty it captured. Its hands dangling at its side, the claws stretched toward the floor in a black display of power. It was of another world, yet it was of her, too, she realized, as the scream escaped her lips and she took off down the hallway.

It did not move at first. She heard no footsteps. For a quick moment, she wondered if she'd imagined it. She turned to look over her shoulder, to see if her wild mind had invented the figure again. But as she turned, her worst fears were confirmed.

It stood still, frozen, right where she'd left it—with one difference. Its hand was outstretched, its claw pointing toward her.

For all of the difficulties she'd been through, for the grief weighing on her, she realized in that split-second a reality she hadn't claimed in the past year. She didn't want to die. She wanted to live.

You know who can help you, Mi. Save yourself. It's not your fault.

The voice was a whisper against the ear-splitting sound. It was as if her voice lilted within the noise now, a familiar warmth in hell. The siren's song worked, loosening her from her frozen stature.

She had to try. She needed to escape. She dashed for her room, terrified she would be clawed to death before she could reach it. Her ragged breath coupled with the painful noise echoing in the house made her movements heavy, disjointed. But when her hand felt the metallic doorknob, she knew there was hope. Running to the window, she fought with the lock on the window, her hands trembling as she lifted it. There was no time to spare, but a thought occurred to her.

She needed to grab one thing, even if it killed her.

Her hands found the familiar leather tucked in the top drawer of her desk. It was foolish to stop. But she glanced in her doorway. The Flayed One was not there. Was it stuck in the kitchen? Would it wait for her parents?

Questions swirled as her body leaped into action. Out the window she dove, landing in a crumpled mass on the ground below. Her legs ached, but she stumbled to her feet, clutching the journal to her chest. She ran onward, not even stopping to see if it had followed her. She didn't have time to consider it.

She was terrified it would follow her. She was leading the big bad wolf right to Grandmother's house. But the little girl inside of her screamed for those warm arms, for safety. She had to try. She had to try to live. She needed help—help that no one could offer her for the past year. No one except one woman. Perhaps her grandmother could save her again.

Her feet pounded on the dusty path, and she slowly noticed the sound fading. The smell was only a subtle odor in her memory, a wisp of truth in her nostrils.

She ran on until the familiar porch welcomed her. Despite everything, she paused for a moment to take in the sight.

Home. Safety. Acceptance.

As she ran up the steps on her grandmother's porch and pounded on the door, the Great Dane inside already howling out a warning of her arrival, she knew she should've come to her grandmother all along.

Chapter Twenty-Two

"We know you've been seeing her," Mia Rose's father began, a biting edge to his already gruff voice. Her interactions with her father were always limited—her mother carried the weight of the family emotionally. So the fact that he was involved said everything.

This was serious.

Mia Rose stood defiantly straight. She had *been seeing her*. She wouldn't stop.

She'd told herself to be brave, to own up to it. She told herself what they thought didn't matter. This wouldn't be her entire life. Soon enough, she'd leave this town and never come back. Her mother wouldn't make the decisions for her any longer, and her father wouldn't be the backbone of her mother's decisions. She would be out in the world, free to be who she was and do what she wanted. Free to love who she wanted.

With an icy inhale, she steadied her resolve and stared straight into her parents' eyes.

"I love her," she said, wishing her words had ricocheted with confidence off the cabinets, the walls, the ceiling. Instead, they were a lilted phrase that hung in purgatory between them all.

"What?" her mother asked, her voice quiet and biting. She stepped towards Mia Rose. The girl forced herself to stay still.

"I said I love her," she repeated, standing a hair taller this time.

Her mother slapped her before she could even think to anticipate it. Her cheek seared with pain. She slouched down, backing up and away from her statement.

"You do not. You won't do this to us, you rebellious bitch. Why do you insist on causing issues for this family? Why can't you just be a nice girl."

"It's not the 1950s, Mother. I can love who I want." It felt good to say the biting words, to defend herself.

"In this house, you can't. I won't watch you go down this path. I won't. Don't ruin your whole life for a phase."

Her mother disappeared down the hallway. It wasn't like her to back off from a fight, especially with her daughter. But perhaps her words had shaken her.

Now, it was just her father standing before her.

"You'll kill her, you know," Dad said now, his mustache wriggling as he shook his head. "You'll kill her with this."

"I hardly think Mother is the weak type," Mia replied.

"Not her. Your grandmother. She's from a different time. A time when this sort of thing wasn't okay. Why do you think your mother feels the way she does?"

Mia Rose paused, her heart sinking. She hadn't considered—could it be? Her grandmother loved her. She would want her to be happy. But her father's words planted something more dangerous than hate, than rejection.

They rooted doubt in the center of Mia Rose's core, an invasive weed ready to overtake everything in its way. Her father turned and plodded down the hallway. His deep consolations of her mother were heard as a fitful cry, angry words, and threats rang out in the house.

She knew her parents wouldn't approve. They didn't like anything they didn't understand, and they hated anything that touted tradition. They hated anything that made them think they didn't have control over her. But she hadn't thought about her grandmother. Maybe her dad was right. Mia Rose started building up the wall that day—the wall of uncertainty. The wall of repressing her feelings, herself.

It would be the wall that would lead to her final coffin in every way that mattered.

Chapter Twenty-Three

"Dear, there you are. Your mother told me you'd be over. Come on, now. I've made dinner."

Mia Rose burst into tears.

"Now, what is it? Come on in and tell me." Her sweet grandmother ushered her inside, and Mia Rose fell into her arms.

"Is the door locked?" she asked, pulling back suddenly. She couldn't be responsible. She wouldn't be.

"Of course. Now, what is it? You're scaring me, Dear. I didn't think you were close to your Great Uncle Mike."

"It's not that. It's worse. Grandma, I can't stay here. I can't. You're in danger if I stay here." She dashed to the windows and drew the blinds, not because it would help, but because it seemed like the logical thing to do. She needed to feel walled in, protected.

"Tell me what's going on," her grandmother ordered in her voice that told Mia Rose she meant business. Mia Rose swiped at her tears and took the seat at the table her grandmother offered.

She didn't have time to be calm and slow about telling the facts. It could cut their time short at any second. But she lingered for another moment in her thoughts, in the knowledge that there would be no going back. She let her grandmother sit in the dark for a moment longer, not wanting to decimate her peace. And then, she reached out and put it on the table.

The little leather journal. The etched letters.

Her grandmother reached for it, mystified and entranced. Her wrinkled, shaking fingers traced over the crude H., the D. Finally, her finger underlined the word Wards as if she couldn't believe her eyes.

"Where did you get this?" she whispered, a reverie in her voice that told Mia Rose everything she needed to know.

"In the woods," she answered honestly. "And I'm in danger because of it."

"I don't understand. It's been so long. He's been gone so long. How?" she asked, shaking her head. Her face winced in pain as if the memories from long ago were too much. She reached across the table and touched Mia Rose's hand, perhaps for comfort.

"I don't either, Grandma. I don't either. But now, you're in danger because of me. Because I'm here."

"Read to me," the old woman said, ignoring the imminent danger Mia Rose spoke of. Ignoring all else. The quest for knowledge was fierce and relentless. Mia Rose gave in and started telling the tale.

JUNE 6TH

There's something living in the forest, something dark and strange.

We've all heard the legends, of course. Edward from the Redwood Asylum supposedly escaped last summer, and rumor has it he is living in the woods behind the stone building. He cries out in the night, a lunatic in every way. He flails and dashes through the wood, naked and uninhibited. He eats rabbits raw and forages for berries to survive. Still, he is mad with hunger and will murder anyone who goes near it.

I won't lie—when I stand out on our porch and stare into those woods, I chill a little bit at the thought. I've always been wary of the woods even though I grew up by them. I never go in there after dark, and I never go far into the dark abyss that is the trees. There have been plenty of times I've sworn I heard something odd past the foliage, something unidentifiable but chilling all the same.

I grew up with the stories that kept most of us out of that forest. For before Edward's escape, there were always stories about the forest between Oakwood and Cedarcrest and how it was haunted. The line between the town sits in the middle of the densely packed trees and overgrown weeds, behind the stone asylum that also haunted my boyhood.

The line is supposedly a dark place. Some say it is a vast stretch that leads to other, hellish worlds when traveled alone. As a young boy, stories flooded through the hallways at the school about those woods. How children were known to disappear there. How the spirits of the tortured souls of the asylum walked the nightmarish grounds and wandered the forest, wanting to exact revenge.

I, of course, am old enough now to understand the origins of these stories. The adults are not as stupid as we'd like to think. I see the tales now for what they were and still are—a ploy to keep curious children and teenagers out of the dangers of the forest and away from the seclusive Redwood Asylum. There are, after all, a lot of secrets in Oakwood that the town would rather keep quiet. There is somewhat of a truce between our two small towns. Oakwood harbors its secrets, and the people nearby in Cedarcrest respect those boundaries. All is well that's kept hidden and quiet—and so we ignore the stories of the lunatics tucked away. We turn a deaf ear to the shrill screams in the night. We pretend the "Psychiatric Hospital," as it's called, is there to help people and not to imprison them.

The stories did work, though. For I never ventured past the tree line in our backyard, even as a curious boy. Even in my days of rebellion and during all of the mistakes I've made in recent years, I did not disobey the unspoken rule: don't go into those woods. I knew what happened to kids who went out there and even some adults.

They disappeared.

Sure, there were the official stories of suicides and runaways. Tales to tell the world and keep suspicions low. But those of us close the scenes, close to those lost knew. We've always known.

There's something much darker at play in those woods. People go to great lengths to protect what is profitable, after all.

There had been at least three over my childhood who were lost in those woods, victims to whatever eerie things lay hidden there. Still, we go on. We heed the tales and the legends all the while pretending we are a normal town, that there is nothing to see here. We do all we can to keep the tourists out.

Rationality tells me those stories, those legends are nothing but fallacies enlarged by the overactive imaginations of children. Still, today, I've started to think there's more at play than I could've ever known. Maybe those legends aren't just protecting the asylum. And maybe the town's elders sway malicious and deceitful.

There is truth in those wild tales. Because after what I saw, I say this—there IS something living in that forest. Last night, I saw it, whatever it was, slinking in the shadows.

I haven't been able to stop thinking about it, my mind clinging to it like an obsessive complex. The gaunt, slim finger slinking through the forest. The piercing cry it emitted. And the smell. Oh, Jesus, the smell, a corpse mixed with mildew, an earthy smell mixed with decay. Vomit rose in my throat and my heart almost exploded as I pulled Dorothy Mae back towards her house. I didn't care if she would get in trouble for sneaking out or if her father would never forgive me for taking his daughter into the forest after midnight. We needed to survive. We needed to get out of there.

She'd taken me for a mad man, swore it was probably just a deer or a wild animal of some sort when I told her there was something odd. But I know this—wild animals don't move like that, upright. They don't smell like that. They don't sound like that. This thing, whatever it was—it wasn't something normal. I'm sure of it.

When we made it back to Dorothy Mae's porch and I could breathe again, I glanced back. The trees swayed in the darkness, and I thought if I sniffed in deeply, I could still sense that vomit-inducing odor. Still, the trees did not give away any of the mysteries. Dorothy's Great Dane, Edmund, scratched at the door, though, barking viciously.

"He never acts like that," she whispered as she giggled. "Damn dog is going to give us away. I love you."

Every hair on my body stood up as I watched the dog wildly attack the door, trying desperately to get out. There was no time to waste, though. We would be caught, and I had to go. So I swiftly kissed her and left her in what I hoped was safety on her porch. Still, as I warily marched down the path between her house and mine, I knew something was very wrong. Something charged the air in a way it hadn't in my seventeen years of living by those woods. Something crept into the air, into the vibrations, into my skin.

There's something living in those woods, all right. Something ominous, just like they say the grounds at Redwood are.

A smart person would steer clear of those woods, like we've been warned to do since we were children. Like we've been scared into doing. But I'm grown now, and I've never been accused of being wise.

So I'm going to go back in. I'm going to figure out what the hell that was lurking in the shadows last night. I'm going to stuff this fear back down into the carcass of my being and figure out what the hell I saw tonight.

I'm going to find out what's lurking in Redwood forest, even if it kills me.

Some mysteries beg to be solved. I know I won't sleep well tonight. The forest is too near for me to get any semblance of sleep, now that I know legends walk after all.

~The Journal of H.D. Wards

Chapter Twenty-Four

When the tears had slowed enough that her grandmother could get words out, she looked up at Mia Rose with shining eyes.

"I loved that boy. I loved him."

Mia Rose could only nod and squeeze her hand.

I loved her, she thought. Two women marred by pain. Two women marred by a broken love. Two women about to be marred by the unknown, Mia Rose thought.

"What happened to him, Grandma?" Mia Rose was terrified to ask. But not knowing was always worse than the knowing part.

"He disappeared. Just gone. Vanished. I spent a year wondering what happened to him. We were in love. We were going to get married that summer. And then poof. No leads. No details. Just gone. They all assumed he ran away. I always thought differently. And now this—"

"Have you seen the creature?" Mia Rose asked, hating to interrupt the story but knowing they needed to get down to business.

"No. H.D. was acting so bizarre right before he disappeared. On edge. Every noise, every twig branch sent him into near hysterics. But I've never seen anything. There are stories, of course. Whispers. But nothing serious."

Mia Rose studied the woman across the table.

"I have." Two words murmured in the safety of the house. Two words to bring them together or tear them apart.

Her grandmother didn't say anything. She just stared. She just listened as Mia Rose told her every detail, every missing event.

When she was done, her grandmother stood. "Come here," she whispered, and Mia Rose fell into the frail woman's arms like she had so many times in her childhood. She let her hold her, stroke her hair, tell her it would be okay even though she was now old enough and wise enough to know promises like that can never be made.

"It's going to be okay. It will."

"I think the creature killed H.D."

Her grandmother exhaled. She was clearly thinking the same.

"We'll figure this out, honey. We will."

"So you believe me?" Mia Rose asked, shocked.

"Of course I do. Why wouldn't I? Just because I haven't seen it doesn't mean it doesn't exist. I can't see my love for you, but it certainly is here, isn't it? Life isn't always about seeing."

Mia Rose closed her eyes, basking in the feeling of unconditional love, a love she'd only ever felt with one other person—and that had turned out to have conditions. She rested against her grandmother, feeling at peace for the first time in days, in weeks, in a year. But after a long moment, she chilled.

Mia Rose pulled back, tears clouding her vision. "I can't risk it coming here. I have to go."

"You will do nothing of the sort, you hear me?" her grandmother ordered, shaking her a little. Edmund, who clearly was not the first of his name, stood up from his resting position, watching the two of them to decide if the quarrel was serious and if he should step in.

"But I can't stay here. What if it comes here?"

"It's all right, Dear. There's nothing to be afraid of," her grandmother whispered in the chilled room, but her voice was uncertain. Her face wore the weary exhaustion of a woman who was both sick and terrified. "I only wish you had come to me sooner. You shouldn't deal with this alone."

Mia Rose shivered. She wanted to believe her grandmother, but she knew some promises couldn't be kept. Edmund whipped towards the door, his back hunched and a low growl rumbling in his throat. The two women looked toward the door, clutching each other closely.

"I'm here for you. Always."

And although Mia Rose took some comfort in knowing her grandmother's words were the truest of true, she could not rest. It would come back. It would come for them, finish the job.

And then who would mourn them? Who would wonder where they had gone to?

They ate dinner, even though neither was hungry. They checked all the doors. They armed themselves with the limited weapons her grandmother had available.

And then, in her grandmother's guest room, Mia Rose finally allowed herself to drift off. Her grandmother insisted on keeping watch at the door to the bedroom, assured her that she would be fine. Mia Rose drifted off holding the dog, her dreams took her to dark places, places that even the creature couldn't touch with its grimy, bloody claw.

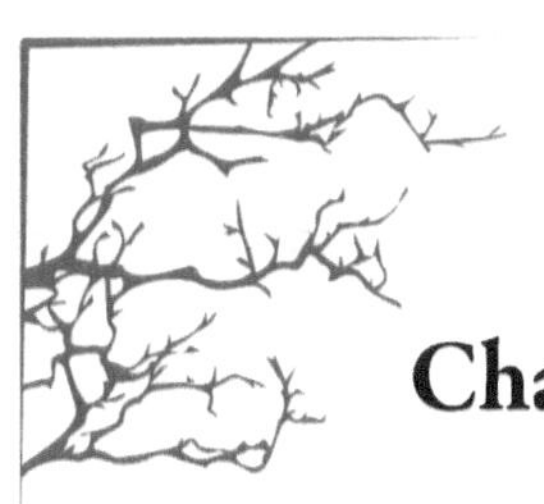

Chapter Twenty-Five

*S*he stared into the mirror, debating on what to do.

On one hand, she no longer cared what her parents thought of her, of the situation. Her heart was hers to own, and they had no right to try to control it. On the other, though, old habits reared their ugly head.

Her desire to make them proud.

Her fear of being rejected.

Her worry that she wasn't good enough, that Lilly would realize eventually what everyone else knew—Mia Rose was nothing special. Was it worth risking it all for Lilly when it probably wouldn't work anyway? She grabbed her phone off her dresser.

Five texts from Lilly.

I need you. Plz meet in our spot. Eight p.m.

Hello? R U coming?

I really need to see you. What's going on?

I'll be waiting in our spot Plz don't be late

Okay, I'm leaving now. I'll see you there.

Her heart leaped in her chest. She almost responded, but what would she say? She needed space, needed time. Needed to mull over her parents' threats, her own fears.

She studied herself in the mirror.

It's one night. One night to come to terms with it all and sort it out. One night of space to make a plan. What difference can one night make? *she thought.*

As eight o'clock ticked by on her clock, thus, she had tucked herself between the sheets to think about it all—the past, the present, and what she wanted it all to look like. She began to drift off, thinking about everything and nothing, thinking about how complex life was after all.

As sleep tempted her, though, she thought about those lips that whispered to her heart, the caress that moved her, and the girl who made her understand exactly what it was all about. She knew what she had to do.

HER TEXTS HAD GONE unanswered, but that was to be expected after she'd ignored Lilly. She hoped she wasn't too late, though. It was almost nine. Certainly, Lilly would have left by that point. Still, she was desperate to try, no matter the cost. Lilly was worth the risk. It was worth the risk, she'd decided.

Her parents had never understood her anyway. She'd always been the black sheep of the family trying desperately to change herself to win their approval. Entering school spelling bees in elementary school just to see her father beam with pride. Taking up ballet for a while in sixth grade so her mom could exclaim what a little lady she was. So many times she'd held back her heart, her thoughts, her feelings for them. Yet none of it mattered. They would never accept her.

Lilly did. Lilly would. Mia Rose marched on.

She got to the clearing, their special spot. The moonlight was thankfully beaming. She looked into the silvery space and saw—nothing. The tall grasses billowed lightly in the summer breeze, but there was no one there. She breathed in for a moment, examining the peace she felt there. She held onto it for a moment, wishing she'd come sooner. She hated that her parents had gotten into her head.

She exhaled and then inhaled once more. An odd scent permeated through her nostrils, one she couldn't quite label. It wormed its way into her hair, into her clothes, into her lungs, and made her cough. It was a foul smell, a harbinger of doom she'd like to push aside.

She checked her phone, although the reception in Redwood Forest was spotty at best. Nothing. She looked back at the familiar path, but a thought struck her.

Lilly was always wanting to take the path by the creek. It was Mia Rose who always insisted they stick to the route they knew so as not to get lost. Perhaps getting lost was what Lilly wanted now. Mia Rose crossed the field and headed to the path toward the right, walking on until the gentle flow of the creek broke into the silence of the night.

The smell had faded now, but she thought she discerned a moaning noise in the distance. Her heart started beating faster, her blood cold. Her stomach dropped as she realized how foolish she had been. She was out in the woods, alone, at night. Who knew what was lurking about, waiting to make her its prey? She trotted on, wrapping her arms around herself.

She stopped on the trail, though, when she saw it. The familiar purple backpack tossed aside beside the path.

"Lilly?" Mia Rose called out into the night, anticipation and terror fighting for dominance. "Lilly?"

The water continued trickling. A branch snapped in the distance. She walked toward the creek, wondering if the wily redhead had decided to dip her toes in. That seemed like something she would do. She made her way through the trees and tall grasses, ignoring the pricks of thorns on her bare legs. She made it to the stony shore of the small creek that ran through the forest, looking first right and then left.

The silver moonlight gleamed off the water—and radiated off a lump in the middle of the water.

Her stomach sank. "Lilly?" she screeched, desperate for her eyes to be playing a trick on her. The red hair was fanned out in the water, a mermaid's mane lapping in the waters. Mia Rose dashed towards her, needing to do something but also knowing in her heart the truth: It was too late.

She rushed to the girl's side, flipping her over. She was cold to the touch. Mia Rose panicked, touching her face, dragging her out of the water. She pumped on her chest, but it was no use. She knew it was no use. But she was not prepared to face the glazed-over eyes, the bloated cheeks, the bluish hue. She could not face it.

It was only when she stepped back for a moment with trembling hands that she saw it. The streams of blood pouring out from the girl's left arm. There were cuts, deep and ugly, up and down her forearm in exactly the right spots.

"What have you done?" she shrieked into the night. "What have I done?"

She crumpled to the ground, sobbing for help. Help did not come. There were no helpers in the Redwood Forest—only regrets, sorrow, and the dark truths of humanity that the town tried to keep hidden.

Her phone had no signal. It was no use anyway. She made her way out of the forest, dragging herself away from the body. Bloodied, wet, and defeated, she traipsed up the stairs of her porch, pounding on the door. When her parents emerged, confused, she crumpled to the ground.

"She's dead. She's really dead."

And then everything faded away. Nothing else mattered except that at that moment, Mia Rose knew that in many ways, she had died, too.

She died, too.

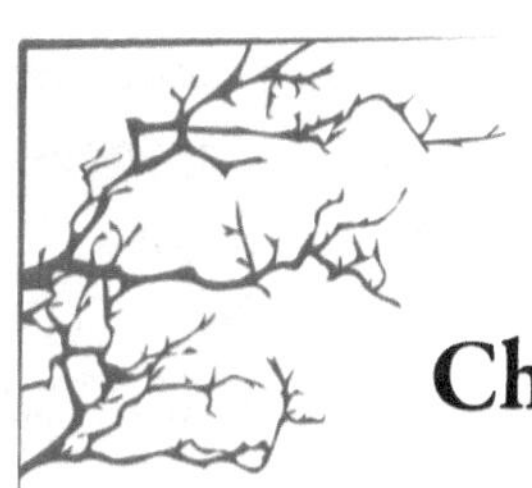

Chapter Twenty-Six

The sun was just rising on a murky morning, a grayish haze cast through the room. As the confusion lifted and her eyes took in the sights around her, fear and relief simultaneously bathed her. She had fallen asleep, despite her best efforts. She hadn't stayed vigilant as she'd planned. All was quiet except for her haggard breathing.

Perhaps the nightmare was over, she thought with swelling of hope. Perhaps it had come full circle when she told her grandmother about the creature. Perhaps...

A chill filled the air as she walked out of the room. Her grandmother was slumped in a chair outside her room, a kitchen knife in her lap. Grayness washed her out, and Mia Rose leaped into action.

"Grandma? Grandma?" she asked, shaking the woman's bone-thin arm as terror usurped her.

Her grandmother rustled, confused and dazed as well.

"Oh, Dear. I must have fallen asleep. Oh no," she cried out, rubbing her neck that was undoubtedly sore from the odd angle her head had been hanging. The woman slowly got to her feet, stumbling to and fro as if unsure what to do. "You're okay. Thank goodness, we're okay."

Mia Rose was about to celebrate the victory as well when her eyes landed on a troubling sight in the living room.

She had thought the house felt chilled when she awoke. And now, a light wind cascaded through the open window in the great room. The drapes billowed, and Mia Rose's heart sank. She did not have to say a word. Her grandmother's wounded whimper told her she had seen the dreaded sight, too.

"Edmund," her grandmother whispered into the air, beckoning her dear friend to her side. But the dog did not come. "Edmund, come." The name was called out with a thickening air of desperation. No pitter-patter of feet, no plodding Great Dane obeyed her order.

Mia Rose steadied her shaking breath, her quaking hands. She stepped forward into the house against all subconscious feelings.

"Mia Rose, no," her grandmother called out, reaching for the girl's arm. Her fingers grazed her sleeve, the pain searing through despite the fabric. She had made the conscientious decision not to show her grandmother her arm. She did not want to trouble her more than she already had. Plus, her grandmother had not required proof of her story, which was valuable on its own.

Mia Rose kept going, disobeying the woman for the greater good. To the window she crept, panic whipping about in her heart, her mind, her chest. Her grandmother cried softly behind her, inching forward on the path she was treading.

The drapes still billowed. Mia Rose told herself to be brave, to be strong, and to face what she must. She stepped up to the window, her hands braced on the bottom ready to pull it down in a pointless attempt at safety. But her eyes glanced out the window and landed on something just at the tree line. She squinted, ascertaining what she thought she saw. Her stomach dropped, realization steadying in her mind. The big, black body did not move. Limp and splayed out, the once glossy fur was tinged with blood. Mia Rose cried out, backing away from the window.

"What is it?"

"Don't," Mia Rose ordered, pointing at her grandmother and ordering her to freeze. It would be too much for her. She could not see it. Mia Rose had yet to even process it herself. How had this happened? When? How hadn't they heard?

Her grandmother, always a strong-willed woman, rushed onward. Upon the sight of her dear friend Edmund mauled and bloodied at the edge of the woods, she collapsed to the ground in racking sobs.

"My boy. My sweet boy," she cried out. "I'm sorry. I should've stayed awake."

Her cries now mixed with the whimpers of Mia Rose, defeated and broken, crumpled on the ground beside her grandmother. They wept for a moment, a painful wail almost drowning out the sound of their ragged breathing.

"It's my fault. I did this." Mia Rose uttered the words after the decimating shock had calmed, after their sobs had slowed.

Her grandmother grabbed her cheeks firmly, her nails digging into her skin. "Listen to me. You didn't do this. That hellish creature did. I will keep you safe, Mia Rose. If it's the last thing I do. Now shut the window."

Her grandmother let go of her cheek to wipe her own tears, to get weakly to her feet, and to help Mia Rose shut the window. She looked out longingly at the body of the deceased as the two locked the window into place.

"I'll kill it," her grandmother whispered defiantly into the quiet space between them. And Mia Rose knew she would—or she'd die trying. She was about to offer to make her grandmother some tea as the two turned from the window, still shaken, when a familiar smell crept about her.

No, no, no, she pleaded with the universe as she clutched onto her grandma, pulling her back. It was too late for prayers or bargains, though. The violent scratching had already ensued at the front door.

Her grandmother put a finger to her lips, demanding her silence. Mia Rose, trembling and horrified at the prospects of what was to come, nodded. Her grandmother yanked her hand and pulled her back into the guest room. Looking around, her grandmother pointed to the closet, the door slightly ajar. Mia Rose shook her head and pleaded with her grandmother. They had to get away. It was their only chance. Still, as she watched her grandmother traipse to the closet, her bones weak and her body failing, Mia Rose knew there was no chance for that. Perhaps there was no chance at all.

Shaky breathing. Arms clasped tight. Her grandmother's clammy, wrinkled hand stroking her arm. Mia Rose whimpered in the darkness of the closet, waiting for death to come. This is where it would end. How badly would it hurt? Would Lilly be waiting there for her like some sappy romance movie? She did not have the wherewithal to consider it as the front door busted open and the smell intensified. The buzzing in her head strengthened. She glanced over at her grandmother. She was whimpering, too, but wasn't holding her head. Couldn't she smell the creature, hear it? What did that mean?

She bit her lip hard, trying to calm herself. Footsteps in the house. A screeching, scratching noise. It would know where they were. It always knew.

Mia Rose took a deep breath. She kissed her grandmother on the cheek. And then she did what she knew she had to do. She stepped out of the closet, into the open, and awaited her doom.

It was already waiting in the room for her.

Chapter Twenty-Seven

It stood motionless, tapping its claws against its leg, the gargantuan creature looming over her with its black, melting body. Up close in the light of day, she understood more fully why the smell was so horrid. Its body oozed and bubbled, the skin flayed open in spots. Pus and black tar seeped from its folds of skin. Whole sections dripped off of its body.

"I'm ready. Take me. Just leave her be," she ordered, her grandmother now standing behind her in terror. She didn't dare glance back though, locking eyes with the creature.

It did not move a muscle, frozen in place as if it weren't even alive.

"Mia Rose, stop, don't," her grandmother pleaded as she marched forward, in front of the girl. She put her arms out in a pitiful but good-willed attempt to shield her granddaughter.

"It wants me, Grandma. Not you. It wants me. Now run."

The creature made a clicking noise with its teeth, its claws tapping again on its leg.

"I love you more than anything. I've lived my life. Go live yours. Now run!" her grandmother bellowed as she did what no one could have expected.

She dove onto the creature, her frail body a weightless feather launched in the air. It batted away her valiant, sacrificial effort with the swipe of a paw, and all three in the room let out a wail that could wake the dead.

Her grandmother lay on the floor, crumpled in the corner. She'd hit her head on the wall, and blood oozed from the place it had scratched her.

Mia Rose stood, incapable of moving. The creature raised its left arm and pointed its rusty, blood-soaked claw at her. She took a step toward her grandmother's dilapidated body. The angle of her neck, though, told her everything she needed to know.

It was useless. Hopeless. Impossible. But Mia Rose did the only thing her body willed her to do. Through racking sobs and exhausted limbs, she fought for her right to live and tell the tale. A right that H.D., Lilly, her grandmother, even Edmund didn't get. She fought for the right to warn others of the maniacal beast haunting their woods. Her feet knew the way, and although she thought for an instant she was dashing into her own grave, she also knew there was no choice. Her feet kept going even though her heart begged her to stop. She did not pause for a breath until she got to the clearing, the place that had, in so many ways, changed everything.

At their tree stump, she allowed herself to crumple to the ground as everything sank in. Her grandmother was dead. It was her fault. It would come for her, too. Good Lord, she hoped it would come for her soon and end everything. She couldn't go on much longer like this.

Swiping at her tears, she clung to the tree stump and forced herself to hold back her sobs. She paused, listening. No ricocheting scream, no putrid smell. It perhaps had stayed behind. It would toy with her later, savoring in the chase a while longer. She reached her hand inside the stump and plucked out the metal box. Her fingers smoothed over the cover before she reached inside.

She flung back the lid, her fingers perusing the collection of objects. The memories swirled around her, the moments both with and without her. She pulled out a picture, the two of them at the arcade. She put on the bracelet from that rebellious day. She pulled out treasure after treasure, a memory box of who they were together. Of who Mia Rose used to be.

And then she froze, her blood running cold yet again.

For at the bottom of the box, inexplicably, unbelievably, was the book that had started it all.

She trembled and gasped, her fingers touching the letters. H.D.

How? How the hell had it gotten there? The last she had seen it was with her grandmother at the table. There was no rational way—

She clasped the book to her chest, wondering if things would've been different if she'd never have found it. Why her? Why had it picked her? She opened the book, fanning through the pages she'd practically memorized.

She flipped to the back of the journal, to the end, and let herself fixate on the final words of the boy who somehow was tied to her.

JUNE 18th

I will go for it tonight. I will stalk into its hunting ground.

I must stop it before it's too late. I can't deal with this pain.

Mama and Dad are making plans. They stalk around me with tension and a quiet resolve. Mama won't look me in the eyes.

I have no time left. I have to stop it before it stops me. I cannot imagine being locked up in the asylum with the beast still lurking. I will have no escape. The thought causes me to shake convulsively. I either end it, or I end myself. At least if I try, I might save others. That's all that matters now.

I am marked. I am gone. But I still can save others.

My knife in hand, it is time to leave. I will take you with me for now. I don't need them having any more ammunition.

And now I go.

The Flayed One lives.

But so does the hunter.

333333333333333

550503363411 End. Those Who Make the Peace Lie.

The words of a madman, perhaps, Mia Rose thought as she tucked the book away. She hadn't solved it. Who could? Perhaps H.D. did belong in the asylum. Perhaps she'd let her grief and isolation carry her down the same path. Except for the creature. Except for its physical presence. Except for her murdered grandmother.

It was real. It was all real. H.D. had most likely died trying to fight it. Or had he escaped? Was he living somewhere, waiting for someone else who had seen what he saw? She had no way of knowing. She had no one to turn to. But she knew one thing—she couldn't stay. Her grandmother was dead. Her parents would be next if she hung around and as much as she disliked them, they didn't deserve to die. Not like that.

She tucked the journal back in the tree stump, a hopefully forgotten relic that would stay a part of her past. She put the other items back except the bracelet. She would leave it all behind. She would be on her own, as she had always been in some ways.

She turned to return home but decided since it would be the last time, she would take a different path. Her feet pointed to the right, towards the river, towards the memorial she could never bear to visit.

It was time to move on.

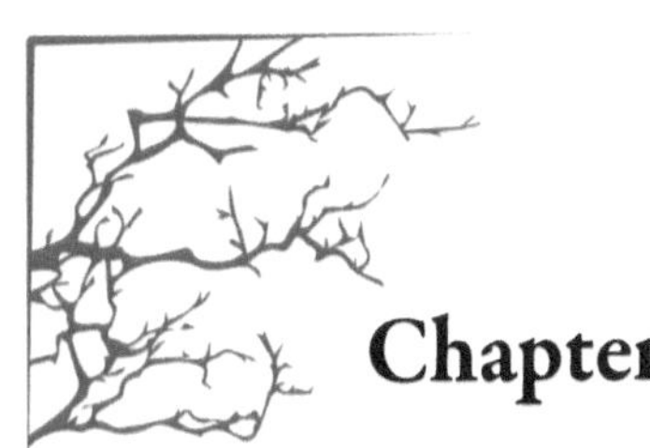

Chapter Twenty-Eight

I saw it again last night. It came like a haunting nightmare. My eyes must have shut for a moment. When I awoke, it was there, a stoic spectral challenging me without a single noise or word.

The nameless creature with the skin dangling from its limbs. The gaunt frame creeping at my window, toying with me like a cat playing with a mouse.

It didn't come in.

I know that it can.

That haunts me in my nightmares, and it haunts me in my waking hours.

There is no peaceful rest anymore.

There is just this hellish torment of knowing yet not knowing entirely.

My skin burns from the inside out. I want to die. I can't live like this anymore.

How does anyone live like this?

~The Journal of H.D. Wards

***

Once in gym class, Mia Rose had tripped and fallen on her face. Her gym teacher, a blobby fellow who smoked too much judging by the stench wafting off of him, laughed and told her she would never be a marathon runner. Now, though, Mia Rose had to take on the role. This marathon was for her life.

She ran on the trail by the river, wanting to inhale Lilly's presence one last time. She would never be able to forget, but time always weakened the ties to the past. A big part of her didn't want to forget. She wanted to breathe in the oaky, muddy scent where her greatest love had breathed her last. What had she been thinking then?

Mia Rose thought she finally understood. The moroseness of being alone, of feeling hopeless, washed over her as she ran past the spot. Her feet automatically slowed in reverence. For a moment, she forgot about the creature lurking about. It didn't matter. She could stop and sit in the river, could let it sweep over her. She could let her black hair fan out in the water, let her body to be found by some other unsuspecting victim.

She leaned on a tree, catching her breath for a moment and staring at the water.

It had been her fault. She hadn't been there for Lilly when it counted. And now it was too late. Too late for everyone.

She had read the words of H.D., had been a witness to his story. But what for? What did it matter? You can't change the past, and dammit, it sure as hell seemed like you couldn't change the future either. She

120

knew that stretched ahead of her were days and days of fatigue and weariness, of monsters of all varieties.

The world was a dark place, and humans were even darker. Behind every monster lurking was a monster wearing flesh. It was hard to believe goodness survived at all.

She thought about ending it all, but in her mind's eye, she heard two voices

One, the voice of a lover who died too young. A wild and reckless lover who taught her to live for herself.

The second, a voice of a beloved elderly woman who had literally sacrificed everything so that she could live.

She could not throw that away, no matter what monster clawed at her. Perhaps that was the reason this had happened. Maybe it was the universe's sick and twisted way of saying Mia Rose Ellis wasn't done living yet.

She took a deep breath of the muddy air, committing it to memory. She exhaled. She turned to the trail that would lead her home to claim her things, and then to the bus stop. The next stop? Who knew?

But as she turned to the trail and breathed in once more, a new smell permeated the air. A foul smell of rotten promises and chaos.

And then, searing pain as her head hit the ground, as it was upon her. As its claws shredded her arm and made rotten meat of her skin.

Her cries echoed out in the forest, but there was no one left to hear her.

The Flayed One feasted on her flesh, finally done with its game.

Her carcass was tossed in the river, a forgotten relic of a girl who once was.

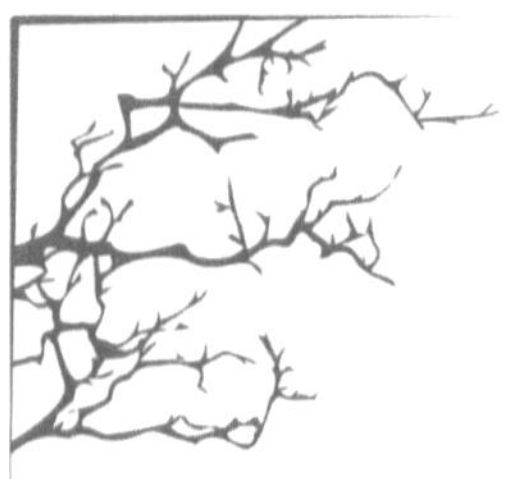

Epilogue

The walls are closing in on her, she is sure of it. She sits on the cot, alone, cold, silent except for the whimpers she cannot hold back. How did she end up here?

She knows exactly how she ended up here.

She was a terrible Mother. And now it was too late. She deserved it all. She deserved it all and then some.

She doesn't know how many days have passed now that she's been here. He stopped visiting her long ago, lost in his own grief of losing a daughter, a mother-in-law, and now her. It couldn't be helped though. She couldn't help it. The death of her mother and the disappearance of her only daughter was too much. Way too much. It had driven her to the point of madness, she knew. A madness that would not unfurl its grip.

She knew what the papers had said. That Mia Rose was psychotic, had finally snapped. With the brutal murder of her mother, suspicions flew. They said it was Mia Rose. Combined with the murder of her lesbian lover the summer before, it was too much. The reputation was ruined. The family was a stain on the town, like so many other families that had gone before them. Some whispered that the town itself was cursed, an evil presence on the loose feasting on chosen residents. At night, when she thought about it all, she sometimes thought they were right.

She wondered sometimes if it was true. If Mia Rose had been responsible. But she'd seen the body of her mother. No girl could do that. No human could do that. She shuddered, thinking of the possibilities. Thinking of the legends, the rumors. Thinking of the tale her daughter had said in the days leading up to it. The creature at her window. The creature in the woods. They'd thought their daughter had lost it, had thought it was the drugs or the psychosis speaking.

Could any of it be true?

She rocked back and forth now. It didn't matter. Mia Rose had disappeared into the night, her body never found. She'd been so caught up in appearances, in not wanting the family to think their daughter had gone crazy. In not wanting them to know her daughter's secret. She'd been blinded by social mores and appearances. She'd forgotten her role as a mother. Now it was too late. Mia Rose was gone.

Had she run away? Was she going to be sentenced to life on the run? That possibility, a lone Bonnie without a Clyde, was perhaps the most comforting one. Because the other possibilities were too much to handle.

Guilt enveloped her, sitting on her chest like a concrete buffalo that couldn't be moved. She would rot away in this hellhole, the asylum she'd always feared as a child. The asylum the children had looked at with intrigue, awe, and terror.

In the room down the hallway, she heard wailing. The blonde girl who used to be a nurse when she first came. She was locked up now. She'd looked at her in the few times they'd passed in the hallways. She'd mouthed one word to her.

Help.

Help wasn't something she could offer though. All she could hope for was a quick death and a punishing afterlife—because a mother who abandons her child deserves no happiness.

She rocked and sobbed, rocked and sobbed, as her eyes landed on the corner of the room.

It stood there, an apparition with an unsettling realness. It had started coming at night. At first, she thought it was the medicine mixture she gorged on every day. Now, though, as she stared at it in the inky darkness of her cell, she had her doubts.

It looked real enough, its long claw pointing at her. And God, the smell. Oh, the smell. The piercing cry it made. She held her head, the tears gushing. But she deserved it all.

She deserved it.

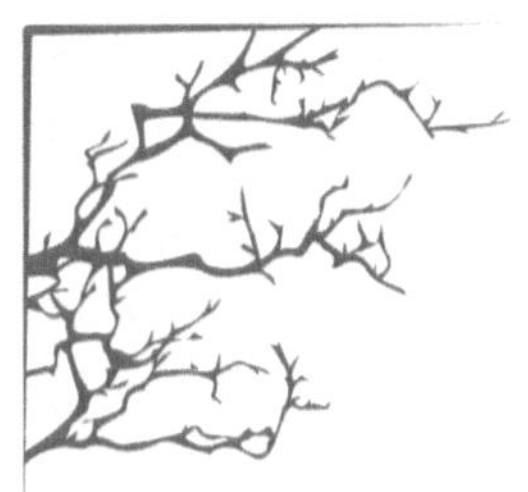

July 2020

The girl flounced into the woods, her phone aimed at the forest as she narrated for her virtual audience. Her perfectly pink pout complimented her glowing skin in a way that attracted a following, in a way that made even a narration of trees exciting.

"So I'm here in Redwood Forest. Don't tell, you guys, but I snuck out. There have been some crazy rumors about a creature or a serial killer living here. A bunch of people have disappeared here, so if I die, you'll all be the witness. Make sure my lipstick collection goes to my best friend Rita, if that happens." Her words were flippant and jovial. Emojis poured in, encouraging her stage presence.

She trod into the forest, adding some jumps and some shrieks for dramatic effect. Her words turned to a whisper as she headed deeper in, dusk falling and casting eerie shadows on her. The crowd watched.

"Last summer, a girl named Mia Rose Ellis is said to have disappeared not too far from here. There was a scandal involving her and another girl, though, so the police thought perhaps she was a runaway. But there are a lot of runaways here in Oakwood and Cedarcrest. A really high number. So I think there's more at play here." Her expert observation stirred a lot of reactions on social media. They bought into the pink pouted beauty. Onward she marched in her sandals not made for hiking. She rattled on about trees and noises, putting on that familiar show for her doting fans.

But then, when she got to a clearing in the woods and started talking about some scene from a vampire movie, the live feed stopped.

Followers grew concerned.

Stories started to spread.

Later that day, though, a new video popped up on her feed. A little glisten from sweat and a bit dirty from her jaunt in the woods, she was armed with a wild story and a journal to back up her ideas. She told of a clearing that smelled horrifically of death. She mentioned a shriek that was earsplitting and chilling. Her pink lips were pale, her glowing skin ashen.

It was as if she had seen something out there. She claimed she had.

And that was when the interest in the journal began, the book she'd found near a tree stump as she had strolled through a clearing.

"This guy is named H.D. Wards, and I don't know...it's freaking creepy, you guys," she uttered into the camera.

She started sharing the journal pages.

The world took notice.

Tales of The Flayed One Spread, and Lucy got her ten minutes of fame.

But now, the journal sits in Lucy's house. There is a dark presence about it, one that forces her to shove it under her bed and eventually into the basement. She doesn't like that book, even though on camera, she laughs it off and plays it up. But no, there's something trouble about those words, those warnings. And more than that, there's something eerie about the dreams she has been having.

Dreams of a girl with black braids. Dreams of a lanky teenage boy with marks on his arms. And dreams of a creature she swears she's never seen but somehow feels like she has.

As the world bubbles about a new monster and the curious of the world seek it out, Lucy hides away in her room, her fingers touching the words of warning.

It comes at night.

She is not ready.

Neither is the world.

Don't miss out!

Visit the website below and you can sign up to receive emails whenever L.A. Detwiler publishes a new book. There's no charge and no obligation.

https://books2read.com/r/B-A-CSYJ-HNNNB

BOOKS 2 READ

Connecting independent readers to independent writers.

Did you love *The Flayed One*? Then you should read *A Tortured Soul*[1] by L.A. Detwiler!

From USA TODAY Bestseller L.A. Detwiler comes a sinister horror with jaw-dropping twists.Everyone has a breaking point.At twenty, an unplanned pregnancy seals Crystal Holt into a marriage to the abusive Richard Connor. After a stillborn birth, Crystal insists they have the baby baptized postmortem. A cynic, a drunk, and a poor man, Richard has other plans. When her monstrous husband tosses the baby into the woods to be forgotten, Crystal instantly spirals. After beating her within an inch of her life, Richard does something else he's done before—he disappears. This time, however, things feel very different...With her husband gone, Crystal battles with the demons of abuse, dark childhood memories, and a declining mental state

1. https://books2read.com/u/b55v5A

2. https://books2read.com/u/b55v5A

worsened by horrific nightmare sequences. As the story unfolds, it becomes clear that something's not quite right about the way Richard disappeared this time, and Crystal is in more danger than ever. After all, not all of the dark secrets belong to Richard.Will Crystal be able to escape from a lifetime of torture unscathed, or will she succumb to the dark secrets she's fallen prey to before?A twisted page-turner that will disturb even the toughest horror and dark thriller fans...

Read more at www.ladetwiler.com.

Also by L.A. Detwiler

The Flayed One
The Journal of H.D. Wards
The Flayed One

Standalone
The Diary of a Serial Killer's Daughter
A Tortured Soul
The Christmas Bell: A Horror Novel
The Redwood Asylum
The Christmas Bell: Rachel's Story
The Arsonist's Handbook
Mr. Alexander Garrick's Traveling Circus

Watch for more at www.ladetwiler.com.

About the Author

L.A. Detwiler is USA TODAY Bestselling author and high school English teacher. Her debut thriller, The Widow Next Door, is a USA Today and International Bestseller with HarperCollins UK/Avon Books. Her second thriller, The One Who Got Away, released in 2020 with HarperCollins UK/One More Chapter. The Diary of a Serial Killer's Daughter released in 2020.

L.A. lives in Pennsylvania with her husband, Chad, their five cats, and their mastiff named Henry. Her writing has appeared in several women's publications and online magazines. She also writes romance under Lindsay Detwiler, including her popular Lines in the Sand Series.

Join her Readers' Club with this link: http://eepurl.com/gkZ2Sf
Read more at www.ladetwiler.com.